The Executioner
and Her Way of Life

Mato Sato

◆◆◆

ILLUSTRATION BY
nilitsu

The
Executioner
and Her Way of Life

CONTENTS

The Executioner
and Her Way of Life
◆◆◆ CRIMSON NIGHTMARE ◆◆◆

4

Mato Sato
◆◆◆

ILLUSTRATION BY
nilitsu

YEN
ON

NEW YORK

The Executioner and Her Way of Life 4

Mato Sato

TRANSLATION BY JENNY MCKEON ❖ COVER ART BY NILITSU

SHOKEI SHOUJO NO IKIRU MICHI (VIRGIN ROAD) Vol. 4
-AKAI AKUMU-
Copyright © 2020 Mato Sato
Illustrations copyright © 2020 nilitsu
All rights reserved.
Original Japanese edition published in 2020 by SB Creative Corp

This English edition is published by arrangement with SB Creative Corp., Tokyo in care of Tuttle-Mori Agency, Inc., Tokyo.

English translation © 2022 by Yen Press, LLC

Yen On
150 West 30th Street, 19th Floor
New York, NY 10001

Visit us at yenpress.com ❖ facebook.com/yenpress ❖ twitter.com/yenpress
yenpress.tumblr.com ❖ instagram.com/yenpress

First Yen On Edition: April 2022

Yen On is an imprint of Yen Press, LLC.
The Yen On name and logo are trademarks of Yen Press, LLC.

Library of Congress Cataloging-in-Publication Data
Names: Sato, Mato, author. | nilitsu, illustrator. | McKeon, Jenny, translator.
Title: The executioner and her way of life / Mato Sato ; illustration by nilitsu ;
    translation by Jenny McKeon.
Other titles: Shokei shoujo no ikiru michi. English
Description: First Yen On edition. | New York, NY : Yen On, 2021–
Identifiers: LCCN 2020054675 | ISBN 9781975319694 (v. 1 ; trade paperback) |
    ISBN 9781975319717 (v. 2 ; trade paperback) | ISBN 9781975335809 (v. 3 ; trade paperback) |
    ISBN 9781975336455 (v. 4 ; trade paperback)
Subjects: CYAC: Adventure and adventurers—Fiction. | Fantasy.
Classification: LCC PZ7.1.S26496 Ex 2021 | DDC [Fic]—dc23
LC record available at https://lccn.loc.gov/2020054675

ISBNs: 978-1-9753-3645-5 (paperback)
       978-1-9753-3646-2 (ebook)

10 9 8 7 6 5 4 3 2 1

LSC-C

Printed in the United States of America

It was one of many endings, the conclusion of a journey long past.

Whiteness, everywhere.

Nothing but pale salt spread in every direction. It was heavier than a white cloud, harsher than a white fog, harder than white sand, purer than white light.

A single sword had turned everything underfoot to powdery dust. As the waves crashed against the coast, the sand slowly melted into the sea, eventually reducing what was once a continent to a solitary island. A moment ago, the island's volume increased by precisely the weight of one teenage girl, but that would only buy a few more seconds.

A single young woman walked along the great expanse of sand that seemed like all the universe's purity manifested into one alabaster world.

She was roughly twenty years old, with dark-red hair that came down to her shoulder blades. Her face was calm and wizened but hadn't yet lost its youth. There was no hint of expression on her face as she strolled in her indigo priestess's robes.

No one would suspect that she had killed someone just moments prior.

As a member of the Faust, who worshipped the Lord, she carried a scripture under her left arm. Because it was a priestess's duty to hold the scripture in her left hand, many of them specialized in one-handed weapons that could be used in their right.

This young woman appeared to be no exception, as she gripped a sword in her right hand.

At a glance, it looked like a very fragile armament indeed.

It was neither elegant nor majestic, nor did it appear practical. The blade was thinner than any rusted or corroded one, brittle enough that it might collapse at a touch or even melt away if it was exposed to rainfall.

The Sword of Salt.

This weapon she carried so casually in her fingers was, in fact, the most terrifying sword in existence. It possessed the power to transform anything its white blade cut into salt.

She had used it minutes earlier to stab an Otherworlder.

Such people were also referred to as lost lambs, for they came from a country called Japan in some faraway world. Each one came bearing a supernatural power called a Pure Concept. Sometimes, they even acquired immortality. They could wield powerful conjurings at the cost of their memories, and if those recollections ran out, they became Human Errors that could effortlessly wipe out an entire city.

Yet even a human with such incredible might could not escape the Sword of Salt.

Yeah, that's as it should be.

Abruptly, the woman thought back to the final moments of the person she slew.

Her victim, who had accepted her inevitable death with a smile, was the closest friend the priestess had ever known. The black-haired maiden had been an insightful intellectual, and she'd loved to mystify people with her words. They'd traveled here together, and now the priestess had killed her own dearest companion.

No conjuring in the world could stop the erosion brought on by the Sword of Salt. It was absolute and irreversible. Excluding water, air, and salt, everything that knew the kiss of its blade crumbled to salt without fail. Not even a Pure Concept holder was immune.

The priestess had brought her all the way here, to the land of salt, in order to kill her. It was for the best. She was an Executioner, a villain. She came here to do what was necessary and had stabbed her friend with the white sword.

"If that's what you've decided, then it's the right choice."

Upon realizing that she would soon become part of this expanse of white, the girl had smiled.

"I'm okay with this being the end, so long as it's your choice. Although… I do hope this is the last time."

And with that, the journey ended.

The girl who had just killed her friend stopped walking.

She was at the center of this island that had once been a continent—the source of the salt erosion that spread endlessly. There, she thrust the Sword of Salt back into its place.

Her task was complete. All that remained was to go back. The priestess turned away, her face still placid, then stopped in her tracks.

A man had appeared in front of her.

He was in his thirties, and his stuffy suit and bowler hat made him very conspicuous. When she considered that this might be his direct response to her friend's silly remark about liking "gentlemen," she felt some degree of pity. Her late friend had been deceitful in many ways.

"Don't tell me...," the man began, his gaze on the Sword of Salt the priestess had just stuck into the ground. Then he looked around, confirming that there was no one else accompanying her, and continued in a tone of disbelief. "Did you...kill her?"

The young woman nodded silently, and the man gritted his teeth in painful regret.

"I see. So we were too late...!"

That wasn't quite true.

They were right on time. He and his friends had arrived precisely when they needed to. If the priestess had waited, then her friend likely wouldn't have died.

That was why she'd ended her life.

Ignorant of that, the man in the stuffy suit spoke with a determined light in his eyes. "...We received word from Ms. Orwell. She's figured out who the Lord really is. As we surmised, the scriptures serve as the Lord's eyes and ears. I doubt she is mistaken."

Evidently, the man had deduced the identity of this world's ruler, learned the true history, and reached the roots of all conjuring. Of course, the priestess did not need to be told any of this. The truth at the heart of this world was utter nonsense, as far as she was concerned.

"We are going to destroy the holy land. With you and Ms. Orwell on our side, we of the Fourth shall create a new world. At the very least, it will be a better one than this—a world where your Otherworlder friend would not have met such a demise!"

Kagarma Dartaros, the Director.

Born without any connection to the Faust and raised without influence from the Elders in the holy land, he'd begun to doubt the structure of society and established an alliance called the Fourth. A brilliant leader, he'd even recruited the young monster of the Commons, Genom Cthulha, and enticed the wandering soldier of the Noblesse, Experion Riverse.

They claimed a new rank in the established order and brandished serious power and enough momentum to move the times forward.

Flare, an Executioner of the Faust, had fought against them several times on this journey, as well as alongside them on occasion.

"Throw aside that which you hold in your left hand. And cast off the clothes you now wear. What good can come of holding on to them any longer? I know you understand. The blasted Elders are of no use to society. Much less their Lord! Just allowing them to continue existing is to stand by and let their corruption spread, which I will never allow!"

His claims were undoubtedly correct.

Yet not one of them resonated with her heart.

"Join us, Flare!"

When he called to her with the nickname she had earned on this journey, her expression changed for the first time.

She scowled in obvious annoyance and looked down.

There was no reason to bother with a reply. After all, she did not feel that the Elders' actions were wrong. They were right in their own way, and most of all, no method genuinely solved the fundamental problems of this world.

Compassion, pity, anger... Whatever he and his men felt, she didn't sympathize in the least.

There was only one thing that concerned her.

Namely, what came "next."

Helping this group wouldn't be enough to stop the "next" thing from coming. Flare was not the first, and she sincerely doubted she would be the last.

This world was utterly hopeless; there was nothing to be done.

How should she deal with this man who so misunderstood her? The answer came from what she held in her right hand.

"*You have new orders,*" sounded a voice from the scripture she carried. Upon hearing it, Kagarma's face froze.

"Flare... Surely, you would not..." The man's voice wavered as he spoke.

Her eyes narrowed, displeased by his reaction. The word *Why?* that seemed to hover in his eyes irritated her. As his lips threatened to form the question, she found herself tempted to tear them apart.

Who in the world did he think she was?

She was an Executioner, down to the marrow of her bones. She was Flare, the murderer.

The scripture in her grip calmly and coldly gave the order.

"*You are to execute him.*"

There was no defying her orders.

The Executioner Flare raised her sword as she had been commanded.

As the train slowed, her consciousness was dragged from the vision back into reality.

She had been dreaming of an old memory.

It had been back before Orwell became the archbishop. When she was still a righteous and upstanding clergy member. Nearly twenty years ago, before the name Flare reached the status of a so-called living legend.

Her mood was sour from the moment she woke up, and the scripture in her left hand spoke to her doubtfully.

"Is something the matter, Master?"

"Just a ridiculous dream, that's all."

Flare scowled at the old thing, which was long past broken.

In the days that followed that event, everyone who'd been involved with the Fourth decayed into twisted shadows of their former selves. That included Orwell herself. The difference between them and Flare was that they had hoped for a better world, while she had never harbored such thoughts to begin with.

"Ridiculous dreams are what made them end up like that in the first place."

The trio who had been the core of the Fourth, Flare the Executioner, and the righteous Orwell.

For just a brief while, five people who would never have customarily interacted had converged and worked more or less together, all because of a single lost lamb.

7

That moment from her dream was undoubtedly when her path broke off from theirs again. They'd been locked in a ten-year struggle ever since.

Flare was confident the others would claim she was the betrayer.

And yet.

"...See?" she muttered. "Here comes the next one."

A pointless past. A memory that didn't even amount to any sentimentality. Even if Master Flare could go back, she wouldn't hesitate to do it all over again. The only part she regretted was missing her chance to kill the Director.

Orwell became the archbishop and fell at the hands of Menou, who was known as Flarette. The fact that Orwell was slain first despite not even being there at the time seemed like a ridiculous irony now.

And now the Director, who had abandoned everything at the end of the bloody battle, had apparently escaped for some reason.

"I don't know what he's playing at, but it's not going to happen."

Surely he had given up long ago, so what was he thinking? Flare watched the afternoon scenery from the train window, but no answers came to her. The pane only reflected her bored-looking face.

She was growing older. After unconsciously comparing her visage in the window to her younger self, she stood, feeling something like depression.

A sulfur-scented wind stirred her dark-red hair when she disembarked the stopped train.

The town she stood in was peaceful and rustic, with unique wooden buildings lining the streets.

"The only thing to do about a crappy dream is to wake up right away."

Master Flare threw back her head and laughed as she set about her sinister machinations.

 # The Escape Begins

When she stepped off the train onto the platform, her first thought was *It's smoky*, but she was mistaken.

The black-haired young woman clutched a train-transfer ticket in her hand as she looked around the multiline station, tilting her head in confusion at the curious sights.

She was a lovely girl, with youthful features better described as "cute" than "beautiful." Her bustline drew the eye toward her blouse, but her overall outfit was elegant and refined, and she wore it entirely naturally.

Akari Tokitou: a lost one summoned from another world, with a frightful power called a Pure Concept attached to her soul.

Her dark eyes, usually full of energy, presently appeared rather gloomy. The hair band that often kept her mussy hair in place was nowhere to be seen, for she had left it in the care of the friend she trusted most in this world.

Akari had insisted on leaving a small token from her possessions with Menou, so that she would know that Akari had departed of her own free will.

With her head slightly lighter than before, Akari peered around through the strange smog.

The floor paved with cobblestones made a satisfying sound at every step. Small but carefully crafted, the platform seemed to be covered in some kind of haze.

But if it were smoke, there would be a smell. And if it were mist, Akari ought to have felt the moisture on her skin. As she looked around for an explanation, she soon realized what it was.

It wasn't any kind of vapor, but tiny, luminous motes.

Guiding Light.

This was the manifestation of the "power" used to create conjurings in this world. Akari searched for the source and quickly found it.

The Guiding trains stopped in the station produced Guiding Light as their steam whistles blared. This phosphorescent glow came from the Guiding engines, which were used to carry passengers. Enough was coming from the train that it made the platform look hazy.

Akari smiled a little at the sight. It was so unlike anything she'd seen in Japan.

She remembered a moment from two months earlier when her traveling companion produced luminous bubbles from a five-*in* coin to make a child happy.

"I wonder what Menou's doing right now..."

Menou was Akari's dear friend. One she'd met in this world. That girl was more important to Akari than anyone or anything else. She'd always been at Akari's side protecting her, but now she was nowhere to be seen.

Akari sighed.

Her nostalgia had shifted into sadness. Trying to shake off the solemn mood, she reached out and grasped the air to see if she could catch the light.

There was no sensation in her palm. The glowing particles displaced by the movement of Akari's hand scattered, fading away like the drifting passage of time.

As she watched the Guiding Light dancing before her eyes, a question arose in the back of her mind.

What exactly *was* Guiding Force anyway?

While the foundation of civilization in Akari's old world was science, the root of most developments in this world was conjuring.

Guiding Force, an energy that didn't exist back on Earth, was such a fundamental aspect of this world that it was part of the definition of life itself. It was the most significant difference between this world and Akari's, and right now, it was floating right in front of her eyes.

A force that leads everything… How did an enigmatic power with such a name become the basis of magic-like conjurings?

Akari was lost in intellectual curiosity for a moment. Then something struck her lightly on the back.

"Bwah?!"

"What are you, a child?"

A small girl two or three years Akari's junior had rudely shoulder charged her. She wore a white priestess robe and snorted when Akari screeched in surprise.

Adorable would undoubtedly be the first word to come to mind upon seeing this girl.

She had shortened the normally ankle-length skirt of her robe significantly and added plenty of frills for good measure.

Her graceful legs were protected from the elements by black tights.

"Unless you're secretly ten years old, please don't play with the Guiding Light. If it's not being used to produce a conjuring of some kind, it doesn't have much physical presence."

The girl's tone was sharp as she scolded Akari for her immature behavior.

Despite her innocent eyes and short stature, her attitude was so openly rude that it made her seem more annoying than endearing. As it happened, her nature was far more aggressive than any initial impression suggested.

"Momo..."

Akari only said her companion's name, but it was enough to make Momo's eyes narrow in annoyance.

Though she was well aware of Momo's real personality, it was still frustrating to be faced with such blatant irritation. Akari's lips twisted into a pout.

Sensing the other girl's anger, Momo glared right up at her from about half a head's length below her line of sight.

"What's that ridiculously babyish expression for, hmm? If you have any complaints, I'd be happy to listen."

"Oh, reeeeally?"

Momo was obviously trying to push her buttons, but Akari had no intention of concealing her animosity, either. She sat down on a bench, folded her arms, and pointedly raised her inflection at the end of her sentences.

"What's the problem? We've still got plenty of time before our connecting train arrives. Why shouldn't I be free to do whatever I want, huh? Besides, it's pretty annoying of you to pick on every little thing I do, Momo. What's the deal? Are you

MATO SATO

a bitter sister-in-law? Perhaps you're jealous that I'm Menou's favorite?"

"Would you mind keeping your fantasies to yourself? After all my hard work planning this trip and making arrangements, the last thing I want to hear is whining from some useless lump. If you can't take responsibility for your own actions, then you obviously aren't free to do as you please, you ridiculous fool. Besides, I don't even want to talk to you, understand?"

"Oh yeeeahhh?"

The exchange grew heated, marking the start of an all-out verbal war.

Akari and Momo scowled at each other with open hostility, the air practically crackling with tension where their gazes met.

The bright and friendly side Akari showed with Menou was nowhere to be seen as she held the sleeve of her billowing white blouse to her mouth and gave a forced giggle.

"Ah-ha-ha! Oh, dear Momo, you're so funny. If you don't want to talk to me, why are you the one who started this conversation in the first place? Forgetting your own actions so quickly suggests that maybe your brain is just as tiny as your body. Oh, sorry. You're sensitive about being short, aren't you?"

"Why, you…"

Akari's uncharacteristic gesture made her insult all the more biting. She'd struck a nerve. Momo's lips thinned, although she didn't drop her adorable smile.

She took a seat on the bench as far from Akari as possible, crossing her legs in their black tights. Meeting Akari's eyes with a sideways glare, Momo smilingly tapped the side of her head with a white gloved finger.

"I'm surprised a Human Error that loses her memories

every time she uses her power is worried about *my* mind. I'd be more concerned about your own brain… Although, I suppose you never had much to work with. Maybe your personality will be a bit more bearable once it goes blank. Then I won't have to worry about my darling quite so much."

"Hah! I pity you, my dear Momo. There's no fixing that nasty disposition of yours. I can't imagine how awful it would be to have to spend your whole life with such a twisted mind in your poor little head. It's silly to worry about Menou when *you're* the one causing problems for her."

"Take care not to talk about my darling when all you have going for you is your ability and those absurd boobs, you useless twit."

"That's rich, coming from a sly little vixen like you. You do realize that Menou doesn't think you're cute the way you really are, right? That's why you always put on the innocent act when you talk to her, huh?"

"Pardon me? I don't want to hear that from a two-faced harlot who would even go so far as to reverse her own memories just to continue acting like a damsel in distress. You little coward!"

The clash of words raged like two blades clanging together. A stormy mood gathered around the pair, darkening the otherwise peaceful platform. Passersby gave the two girls a wide berth.

Momo's tongue was even sharper than usual, honed from sheer animosity. Still, Akari refused to give in.

"*You're* the real coward, aren't you, Momo? You've known Menou since you were little, but you still can't even hold a

natural conversation with her unless you put on a cutesy act…
Is your self-confidence really *that* low?"

"Ah-ha-ha-ha-ha, better than being an airhead who can't
win my darling's heart no matter how many times you repeat
the same events over and over!"

A common goal had brought Momo and Akari together, but
they were neither friends nor comrades. To call them natural
enemies would be an understatement. Their traveling together
meant near-constant disaster.

"Whew. You've got a big stock of insults for someone so
small, Momo."

"And you must store them in that chubby stomach of yours,
I assume."

With that, a cease-fire was called so both sides could catch
their breath.

Perhaps the pair had realized the futility of their fighting?
The nearby crowd waiting for the same train felt a collective
sense of hope, but it proved to be a fleeting one. After a bit, the
girls began glaring daggers at each other again, sparks flying
like a wool sweater being rubbed in the dry winter air.

The silent standoff didn't remain that way for long.

As the tension built rapidly in the air, Akari was the first
one to fire another shot.

She opened with a jab, heaving a loud, deliberate sigh.

"Oh dear. Not getting along with your traveling companion
ruins any enjoyment you might get out of the journey, doesn't
it, dear Momo?"

"What a coincidence. I was just thinking that a journey is far
more taxing with someone absolutely awful."

"Yeah, I totally get that! Finally, we agree on something!"

Although Akari's tone was light, there was enough heat behind every word to singe the eyebrows of nearby listeners. She carried on the cheerful yet unnerving conversation, then suddenly dropped her voice low.

"No wonder Menou always makes sure to travel separately from you, Momo."

At that, a vein popped in Momo's forehead.

The attack had struck her right where it hurt. For a moment, the level of rage she couldn't entirely hide reached a downright murderous level. Yet even as Momo let off an overwhelming air of "I'm going to tear her head off," she maintained a shallow smile.

Akari's calm expression remained firm, too, despite being on the receiving end of murderous intent from someone who had undergone intensive training to become an assistant Executioner.

There must have been an unspoken rule that whoever stopped smiling first was the loser. This was an absurdly meaningless battle of pride.

"The only reason I journey separately from my darling is because some nasty little insect got between us, understaaand? I'm sure every second she spent with me and away from you felt like a breath of fresh air for her."

"You think sooo? It's never once occurred to you that maybe Menou was trying to escape the annoying little stalker who uses her position as an assistant to take sneaky photos of her? Or perhaps you aren't aware of how awful your personality is, Momo? You've got to be aware that you're bothering other people!"

"I'd say you're the one who needs to realize how terrible

©nilitsu

you are. I'm sure it must have been rough for my poor darling to travel with such a nasty, rotten woman."

Unlike the grandiose exchange of insults from the first round, the pair was now using someone who wasn't present to stab at each other. If the person in question could hear this argument, no doubt she would develop an instant headache at the sheer absurdity.

But sadly, there was no one here now to mediate between the two.

"By the way, regarding those so-called sneaky photos, I have an entire album of my darling when she was little. Would you like to see?"

"...?!"

The sudden curveball stunned Akari into silence for the first time since the war began.

A priestess's scripture possessed the ability to record images in the form of a conjuring. Momo had made thorough use of this, as it was one of the few conjurings she excelled at, to create an extensive (and highly unauthorized) album of her beloved Menou from a young age.

Akari was aware of this, as well. Her eyes darted around, revealing her inner conflict about taking the bait.

She wanted desperately to see it, but the last thing she wanted to do was nicely ask Momo to show it to her. Akari had her pride, too. And yet...her feelings clashed, and she groaned in anguish.

Watching Akari's obvious distress, Momo burst out laughing.

"Ah-ha-ha-ha, you are soooo stupiiid! Like I would ever show it to you even if you asked, you idioooot!"

"Whaaa—?! Y-you little…!"

While Momo snickered in a show of laughter that was fitting of her age in a way, Akari glared at her vengefully. Clearly feeling that she had the advantage, Momo shook her head and adopted a pitying tone.

"My darling collection is my most radiant treasure, the result of many years of hard work, you knooow? And besides… My darling herself erased it a little while ago, so it's gone now."

Recalling as much evidently wounded Momo. She suddenly slumped down heavily, covering her face with her hands. Menou had tempted her with the prize of a swimsuit photo, then mercilessly erased the entire collection with her own hand.

"W-wait, it's gone?" Akari seemed equally shocked that she'd lost her chance to see photos of a young Menou.

Incidentally, Momo had yet to notice due to her distress at the time, but Menou only actually erased the photos that were taken without permission. She left any that had been captured normally, out of the goodness of her heart.

"Okay, but—ugh."

As the pair attempted to recover from their mutual shock to resume exchanging insults again, a bell rang, indicating the arrival of a train.

It was the one they were scheduled to take next, gliding into the station with the heavy chugging of wheels. The boisterous sounds of its arrival forced Momo and Akari's arguing to quiet.

Both of them were still grappling with regret over the insults they had yet to unleash. While each girl wore an expression that said *I was just getting started*, they weren't foolish enough to risk missing their train over it.

"...Hey, Momo. The thing you said before we left the oasis was true, right?" Akari asked.

"Of course it was. I have no reason to lie about that. Why else would I bother bringing you along with me?"

Instead of fighting, they spoke about their next moves.

Akari had parted with Menou, her most precious friend in the world. Momo, too, had taken Akari away despite knowing it would upset the person dearer to her than any other.

The two girls stood to board the train. There was only one reason they were leaving Menou behind.

So that she would survive.

"As long as my darling is chasing us, she will never betray the Faust."

That was why the pair was traveling together, even though they couldn't get along by any stretch of the imagination. Getting far away from Menou was the most important goal.

"And you're sure Menou isn't going to catch up to us?"

"But of course. We have a three-day head start on my darling, after all."

"Three days?"

"Did you think I left my darling's side without taking any cautionary measures?" Momo clearly didn't care to reassure Akari, but she explained anyway. "Before we departed the oasis, I stole all her travel funds. She'll be too busy raising funds to come chasing after us."

"...Yikes." Akari looked taken aback by her heartless method. "You really are a nasty one, Momo."

"Of course I am," Momo responded coolly. "There's no such thing as a nice Executioner, except for my darling."

Akari had no response to that strangely convincing argument.

With each gust of wind, the sands of the Wild Frontier's desert danced in the arid atmosphere. The sun constantly burned the skin in this harsh climate.

At the center of this unforgiving desert, the oasis was a crucial rest area that provided water and respite from the intense surroundings. In addition to quenching one's thirst, the abundant water source fostered lush greenery that was otherwise scarce in the desert. People gathered there and made buildings. Before long, it became a valuable stopping point on any desert journey.

Presently, one lone girl stood in a tavern in this town.

Despite being in her midteens, she possessed mature beauty and was clad in the indigo robes that marked her as an official priestess. There was a generous slit in the right side of her skirt, but it wasn't there to show off her long, slender legs; it was so she could easily access the dagger kept in a belt around her thighs.

Her name was Menou, also known as Flarette, and she was a taboo-hunting Executioner of the Faust.

The girl's entire body was glowing with phosphorescent Guiding Light. Her spirit never wavered, even in the span of a single breath.

She drew out "power" from her soul, controlled it with her spirit, and circulated it through her entire body. While the Guiding Force was flowing into her flesh, it stagnated and stalled unnaturally in some areas. She focused on returning these problem areas to normal, slowly maintaining the distribution.

Menou had taken considerable damage in recent fights.

First, she'd battled the armed criminal group Iron Chain. Then Sahara, the nun with the artificial arm. And finally, she'd combated the wish-fulfillment puppet that Sahara's hopes brought to life, the Primary Triad conjured soldier.

She'd managed to emerge victorious from the fearsome battles, but certainly not unharmed.

The injuries from the final conflict were particularly intense. Menou had recovered in the last moment from very near defeat. Now the priestess was concentrating on mending her wounds.

Guiding Enhancement strengthened the user's physical capabilities. She was using it to focus on enhancing her body's ability to heal, hastening the process of closing her wounds. This method could restore injuries swiftly, although it did have its limits.

After a while, Menou's eyes flashed open.

The Guiding Light surrounding her body dissipated. With a short sigh, she stood up and shook out her limbs. As she stretched, her tawny-brown ponytail swayed along with the black scarf ribbon holding it in place.

After a series of movements to check whether there was any pain remaining, she determined there were no significant problems.

"Yes, that should do it."

Menou wasn't back to her full strength, but she had recovered to the point where she felt prepared for a fight. Most of the damage she'd sustained had been skin-deep, which was easier to mend. It wouldn't be so easy to heal if they were bone fractures, cuts that reached internal organs, or other more severe injuries.

"Now, that takes care of my health…," Menou trailed off, then lowered her tone. "But I have to do something about the money."

Her eyes were full of anguish as she gazed at the bed, where all her travel belongings lay.

The sturdy leather bag that usually hung off her belt was flat, starved of its usual contents. She had spread out everything she carried with her on the bed so she could look it all over with an objective eye.

As Menou stared at the neatly arranged personal effects, her expression soured further.

With everything out in the open, it was all the more apparent. The most important item she needed for her travels was missing.

In short, her money was gone.

"…Why in the world would this happen?"

Menou held the empty purse between her fingers. The nature of her sadness was strangely specific: that of one all too acquainted with the anxiety of living without funds.

She had saved up to pay for travel expenses by taking on missions—and at other times by undergoing outrageous tribulations—and now it was gone. Menou hadn't wasted it all on an extravagant shopping spree. That much was certain. In fact, she was accustomed to a frugal and diligent lifestyle. Just the other day, she had taken down the criminal group Iron Chain in their desert hideout as part of her work for the Faust.

Yet while she was off getting caught up in all kinds of trouble, someone had broken into her room at the inn and stolen all her money.

As a priestess, Menou was familiar with honorable poverty, but she certainly didn't enjoy it. Technically, she was an elite who had worked her way up the ranks in the clergy; why did she have to suffer so in the name of funds? Her thoughts wandered to such escapist musings because money was not the only thing she'd lost.

Something else had been snatched away.

Akari Tokitou, who she'd been traveling with all this time, was missing.

As Menou was forced to grapple with her dire straits again, she muttered darkly to herself, "I feel a headache coming on..."

This was an even bigger problem than the empty purse. In fact, the girl's disappearance was so serious that being broke was trivial by comparison.

After all, Menou's current role was to travel with Akari.

Akari Tokitou was a lost lamb summoned from a country called Japan in another world, and she was the holder of the Pure Concept *Time*. Menou's job as an Executioner was to supervise and eventually deal with her. But now her target was gone.

Menou folded her arms, wondering what to do, when a voice suddenly rang out behind her.

"Wow, talk about pathetic."

She turned around, but there was no one there, only two scriptures sitting on top of a table. Momo had left one behind, but the other was the source of the oddity.

Menou's personal scripture was speaking in a human voice.

"How's it feel to get outwitted by your own assistant?"

"Don't be ridiculous, Sahara."

As soon as Menou coolly spoke the name of the voice's owner, the scripture emitted Guiding Light that formed a holographic image.

A girl in a nun's habit appeared floating in the air.

Her wavy silver hair came down to just above her shoulders, while her half-closed eyes gave her a permanently listless expression. She was undoubtedly a beautiful young girl, but her most eye-catching feature was definitely her size.

She was small enough to fit in the palm of one's hand.

Although she originally belonged to the church, the girl harbored jealousy and envy toward Menou that had driven her to use taboos. She'd lost her body after a fight with Menou, yet somehow, her spirit had ended up within Menou's scripture in a strange twist of fate.

Depressed over the awful surprise, Sahara had spent a while curled up in a ball muttering *"I want to die"* over and over, but she started getting livelier upon seeing what Momo had done to Menou.

"Momo took poor Akari away. Your trusted assistant has betrayed you, Menou."

"...We still don't know for sure that Momo's responsible."

"Yeah, right. I'm sure you're fully aware it's the most likely possibility."

"......"

Menou fell into dejected silence.

Sahara was correct. The signs that Momo had absconded with Akari of her own free will were painfully apparent. Akari's hair band and Momo's scripture had been left behind. Throw in the note, and there was no doubt that the two girls had chosen to leave. Menou suggested otherwise only to cover for her friend.

"What are you going to do? This decision doesn't make any sense for an Executioner's assistant. If you ask me, you obviously have to report that violent little freak show as a traitor to the cause, y'know?"

"I'm not going to do that. I'm sure she has a good reason for her actions. Besides, she's my assistant. I have to take responsibility for her."

"...Ugh. It's so typical of you to be soft on Momo; it gives me the chills."

Menou coolly ignored Sahara's jab. "Too bad. This development means I'll have to deal with you later."

Momo's deed couldn't be ignored. So for now, disposing of Sahara as a nun who had committed major taboos would have to wait.

Menou rapped on the scripture lightly with her knuckle.

"Sahara. Right now, you are a taboo. I'm sorry, but I have no way of saving you. Maybe you should be grateful to Momo for extending your life span?"

This time, it was Sahara who fell silent at the snide remark.

Even if the Mechanical Society had influenced her, her actions were unpardonable.

On top of trying to kill Menou, she was fused to her scripture due to taking on the characteristics of the Mechanical Society. Sahara's very existence was now taboo.

She had transformed from a human into a Guiding Force life-form.

Losing one's body while keeping their soul and spirit preserved was a rare phenomenon. Once Menou caught up with

Momo and restrained her, she would have to take care of this situation with Sahara, too. She intended to offer the scripture containing Sahara as proof when she reported the incident.

"I was planning to hand you over at the church in the next town, but I have no time for that now. Once I get Momo back, I'll just have to carry you with me all the way to the holy land."

To reach her destination and the Sword of Salt, Menou would have to traverse the holy land, the central location of the Faust. Making that trip had become a necessity from the moment she had chosen the Sword of Salt as her means of slaying Akari, who was not killable by standard methods.

"Whatever they do with you after that is none of my business... I imagine you may want to prepare for the worst."

Menou only refrained from burning her scripture to be rid of Sahara because she didn't really understand what exactly the former nun had become.

All she knew was that Sahara's presence in the scripture hindered Menou's ability to use conjurings. For now, she would have to borrow the one Momo had left behind.

"I'll need you to stay out of sight until then. No taking on a visible form with Guiding Light, obviously—and try not to talk at all, either."

"...And if I refuse?"

"Then I may have to consider destroying you on the spot."

It was rare for a human to transform into a Guiding Force life-form but not completely unheard of. Still, it was baffling that Sahara somehow existed within Menou's scripture.

One of the main reasons Menou didn't torch the book on the spot was that there was no telling whether it would worsen the situation. It might even cause the wish-fulfillment puppet to appear again.

That scenario seemed highly unlikely, however.

In truth, a small amount of sympathy for Sahara and reluctance to kill her a second time also helped to stay Menou's hand.

"...I see."

Sahara sounded unfazed by this threat of execution.

"Do whatever you want. I don't intend to help you, and I certainly don't want you to help me, either. I am a former nun who committed a taboo. You are an Executioner priestess who disposes of people like me. That's all there is to it."

"...True enough."

If that was how Sahara felt, there was nothing more Menou could do. At most, she could offer her someone to talk to, and even that was only for the short time until Sahara was gone for good.

"Either way, I still have to go after Momo first. I need to know what she was thinking when she took Akari away, after all."

"How? You don't exactly seem like you're in great shape to catch up to anyone right now."

Sahara looked at Menou's empty purse and smirked.

"I mean, you don't have any money, right?"

"No, I suppose not..."

She was absolutely right. This fundamental problem had to be solved before Menou could take any further action.

Of course, she wasn't without any plans to deal with that. Menou knelt down and slipped a hand into her calf-length boots.

The rustle of paper money brushed against her fingertips. She grabbed it and pulled out a ten-thousand-*in* banknote.

"...*I guess you're not totally broke, then.*"

"Naturally. I've been traveling for a long time, you know."

Sahara sounded disappointed, but Menou ignored that.

The priestess wasn't foolish enough to put all her funds in a tiny purse. She still had the small amount she'd broken up and hidden on her person. It didn't amount to much, but it should have been sufficient to buy food and water to get through the desert.

"*It's still not enough, though.*"

Sahara was right again.

If Menou crossed the desert with so little, she would run out entirely by the time she reached the border. If Momo hoped to escape pursuit, she would probably ride a train, and if Menou took on a job to raise travel funds, she would miss her chance to catch up to Momo and Akari.

Generally, when Executioners like Menou needed to borrow money for their missions, they were tasked with resolving local difficulties. Since they were outsiders to the parish, it was accepted that they would have to work to earn their budget.

Even if Menou made it to the next town, there was no guarantee that the church there would simply hand over the capital she needed. She would definitely lose Momo and Akari's trail if she wasted extra time negotiating.

Menou tapped the banknote against her chin in thought.

What was Momo's reason for taking Akari away?

She had kidnapped Akari while Menou was fighting Iron Chain and even went so far as to steal Menou's money to slow her chase. The sudden turn of events was like a bolt from the blue to the Executioner.

Menou and Momo were very close. They had known each other since their childhood in the monastery. Surely the kinship they'd built over the years wasn't all in Menou's mind.

Then why would Momo go against Menou's orders and take Akari away?

Menou searched her memory for any moments that might explain the behavior, and she found them.

"Since this mission involves being with the target for an extended period, please let me do it instead... I don't think this mission...suits you, darling."

"...But that's not exactly what I'm worried about, you knooow."

The conversation was from when Menou first undertook the journey with Akari: in Grisarika Kingdom, when she first realized her role. At the time, Momo doubted whether Menou was suited for the job.

Two months had passed since then.

"...So that's how Momo saw things," Menou whispered to herself, so quietly that even Sahara couldn't hear her.

She faintly understood why Momo had made an unauthorized judgment call, but it only made her frown deepen.

Momo was exceptionally skilled. However, her thought process could be a bit self-absorbed, likely because she could solve most problems simply by relying on her sheer strength and capability. Her fundamental approach was to rectify issues however she saw fit. The girl rarely considered methods that didn't come naturally to her.

Consequently, this made her easy to predict.

Her work in the field was incredible, but she was far too

picky when forming plans. While Momo obediently followed Menou's orders when she was under her direct supervision, the fact that she struggled with sticking to those commands in any other circumstances was the reason she remained an assistant.

It was easy to guess why she'd stolen the travel money. It was to slow Menou down, plain and simple.

When traveling with someone as inexperienced as Akari, it naturally took much more time to get from one place to another. Momo had to buy time to prevent Menou from catching up to her.

There was an easy way to get around this, however.

"I'm guessing it would never even occur to Momo that I might ask *that* person for help."

"*What person?*"

Sahara was unaware of who Menou was referring to.

"I happen to know someone with deep pockets, you see."

"Money? But of course."

The person Menou sought travel funds from readily agreed before a number was even mentioned.

This generous figure also happened to be a gorgeous one. She was quite tall for a woman, endowed with all the right curves and wearing a remarkably skimpy dress that accentuated them all. Even without any ornamentation, she was already strikingly beautiful. Few people could boast a noble upbringing, natural features, and personality that matched so well.

Her name was Ashuna Grisarika, the mighty young Princess Knight of Grisarika Kingdom.

She had fought alongside Menou during the operation to destroy the criminal group Iron Chain. Ashuna had taken no small amount of damage in the struggle, but there were no visible scars on her now. Most likely, she had used Guiding Enhancement to hasten her healing along just like Menou.

"Are you certain? I haven't even said how much I need yet."

"It does not matter."

Ashuna crossed her legs and smiled elegantly, her blue eyes twinkling.

"If lending you money will put you in my debt, I could ask for nothing more. Go on, give me a number. The more digits, the better. Ideally, an amount you could never possibly pay back."

"...I'd prefer to borrow the absolute minimum necessary, thank you very much. I will reimburse you as quickly as possible."

"Really? Well, that's too bad."

Ashuna looked genuinely disappointed. She didn't lend because she cared little for her fortune, but because she knew that Menou was an investment guaranteed to yield a good return. The debt would be settled by Ashuna collecting Menou herself, and this eagerness clearly made the priestess visibly uncomfortable.

Ashuna didn't seem particularly bothered by this. She just tossed her purse casually over to Menou.

"Here, take as much as you want."

"...Thank you."

Menou was well aware of Ashuna's gallant personality and that it was better not to protest. Thus, she simply took a few ten-thousand-*in* banknotes from the purse on the spot.

"If all you require is such a trivial amount that can be contained in one purse, simply borrowing and returning it would provide little entertainment. This is a rare chance. Perhaps I should attach some conditions?"

"I wasn't borrowing money for your entertainment, but…all right. Will you require interest or something?"

"Interest? Where's the fun in that?"

Charging interest was a standard tactic for lending money. While the ever-parsimonious Menou worried about whether it would be too excessive, a wicked grin spread across Ashuna's face as she accepted the purse back.

"Hrm, so you only borrowed fifty thousand *in* or so? No need to reimburse me, then. Instead, I will have you do something amusing for me."

In spite of being told she didn't have to pay the money back, Menou's fears only doubled.

She watched and listened with growing dread as Ashuna stood.

"As you may be aware, I have a fondness for clothes."

"Yes, well, I suppose that makes sense."

The dress Ashuna usually wore possessed a unique and innovative design. It was easy to surmise that the woman was particular about fashion.

But what did that have to do with her terms for lending money? As Menou struggled to see the connection, Ashuna strode over to a closet in one corner of the room.

The closet was full of all kinds of garments.

Ashuna's dress was indeed remarkable, but the other ensembles in her wardrobe spoke to her fondness of finery, too. Ashuna picked one out with a wolfish smile.

"Here you are, Menou. I will ask you to wear this for a while. Ah, worry not, I shall have my tailor adjust it to your size."

"...Excuse me? You want me to wear *this*?"

Looking at the outfit she'd been handed, Menou couldn't stop a rare expression of being dumbfounded from crossing her face.

Few territories on this continent had a large enough population and area to be called a nation.

The environment made consistent survival difficult for humanity due to dangerous monsters, powerful conjured soldiers, and most of all, the aftermath of the Human Errors. Since every nation was surrounded on its borders by the Wild Frontier, most of the denizens of this world would never even consider traveling from one country to another.

If there was ever a reason for ordinary citizens to consider venturing through these perilous regions, it was to go on a pilgrimage to the holy land at the west of the continent. Since there was a great deal of risk involved in traversing the Wild Frontier, most people would only attempt the journey once in their lives, if even that.

This is why most humans in this world referred only to moving within their homeland when they spoke of traveling.

The Guiding trains were indispensable for transportation over any area that was at least relatively safe. Tracks were laid out within every country, making them humanity's most popular form of voyaging.

The locomotive that ran across the plains past the desert at the continent's center and toward the mountainous region was also used for domestic trips.

Its interior design was simplistic. There was an aisle through the middle of each car, with seats lining the left and right sides. The red cloth-covered chairs looked comfortable but actually did very little to protect the passengers from feeling the framework of the train. Since they were designed with only appearance in mind and no actual cushioning, sitting on them for a long time meant that one would feel the shaking of the train enough to leave their bottom sore. The seats were infamous for their discomfort.

Momo and Akari were in two such chairs, chatting about Menou to pass the time.

"I know Menou always wears her priestess robes, but she looks great in anything, don't you think? It's amazing how she can be that cool but still pull off cute clothes just as well. I still remember that maid outfit she was wearing when we first met. It was so frilly yet simple and adorable! ...Have *you* ever seen Menou in attire like that, Momo?"

"You mean the one from Grisarika Kingdom? Obviously, I haaave. I'm the one who created that maid outfit, you knooow! Thanks ever so much for the compliment, you fooool!"

"Whaaat?! You can make stuff like that? Dang it, I don't have those skills..."

"But of cooourse. I've been recording my darling's growth and fashion since we were little, and I spare no effort for her sake. Unlike a certain someone who probably can't even cook, or sew, or infiltrate and search a place, or take out small-fry in battle, hmmm?"

"Grrrr...!"

One was an assistant priestess raised in a monastery in the holy land; the other was a lost one from another world. With two vastly different personalities and sets of experience, the pair had nothing else in common to discuss except Menou. And as it happened, Menou was the topic both of them were interested in most.

Although they were reluctant to acknowledge it, the pair had plenty to converse on when it came to Menou.

"Speaking of Menou's fashion, you mentioned before we got on the train that your records got deleted... Are you sure they're all gone, though? Scriptures can record pictures and stuff, right? Menou is really nice deep down, so I doubt she would erase all your treasured memories. This means I still have a chance to see a young Menou! Am I wrong?"

"Now that you mention it, I suppose some of the usual pictures might still be intact...but I left my scripture with my darling. So either way, I have nothing to show you."

"Aw, come on. Wait, why did you leave your scripture with her in the first place? Isn't that thing a weapon?"

"I rarely use my scripture in battle. Besides, scriptures that are linked for communication can also locate one another if they're in close enough range. Menou could use that to find us, so I had to leave it behind."

"Hmph. Thanks for nothing, Momo!"

"Be quiet, you useless girl." Looking satisfied with the silly advantage of being the only one who had known Menou as a child, Momo folded her arms smugly and changed the subject. "Now then, since we have time on our hands, let's talk about something else."

"C'mooon, what could be more important than pictures of Menou as a kid?"

"Give it up. Even if I had my scripture, I would never show them to you. We're changing topics, okay? I have questions about your memories."

A few other passengers were riding in the same car as the two young women. Momo glanced around to confirm that they had no unwanted listeners, then kept her voice low enough to be lost amid the sounds of the running train as she brought up the topic they discussed almost as often as insulting each other.

"You used your Pure Concept conjuring to *Regress* time for the entire world, with my darling's death as the trigger. That's correct, yes?"

"Mm-hmm."

Akari Tokitou had the Pure Concept *Time* attached to her soul.

As the name implied, Pure Concepts were superhuman conjurings that enabled the user to control an entire concept. There were many other varieties besides Akari's *Time.*

The people of this world sometimes summoned Other-worlders searching for this incredible power, although they occasionally wandered in naturally, too.

It was the role of Executioners like Momo and Menou to slay such taboos, but this time, the circumstances were different.

"And you said you've been turning back time over and over in search of a way to save my darling from dying on the journey to the Sword of Salt, yes?"

Akari nodded silently but intently.

Momo leaned back in her seat. It looked soft to the eye, but that was firmly limited to its appearance. Little more than a thin layer of cloth wrapped around hard wood, the seats directly conveyed every last rattle of the train to anyone unfortunate enough to be sitting in them.

As the locomotive rocked around, Momo gathered her thoughts again.

Turning back time for the entire world.

It was difficult to imagine just how this phenomenon functioned. The effect was massive, and there were no records of anything similar. Momo had no way of observing what happened to the time line when it was turned back, either, meaning there was little use theorizing about it.

Only one thing was for sure—the *Regression* always worked out in Akari's favor.

She was the one with the Pure Concept, the person actually using it. The resulting occurrence was bound to obey her will.

"You are truly an absolute thorn in my side. Your entire existence is unbelievably inconvenient."

"Right back at you. Besides, I'm only stuck turning back time because *you* can never protect Menou, got it?"

"Complaining about a version of me from a time I've never experienced means nothing to me, idiot."

Until Momo heard Akari's side of the story, she had been acting solely to support Menou, fully supporting her decision to use the Sword of Salt to kill Akari.

Yet as soon as she learned that Menou had betrayed the Faust to protect Akari in a previous time line, Momo's goal changed.

Even before that, she'd had her concerns.

Menou was an incredibly skilled Executioner. She always killed her targets after a concise period of interaction. Her methods echoed those of Flare, the one who had taught her and Momo. Indeed, Menou was now known as Flarette in certain circles of the underworld.

But because Menou was so skilled, she invariably slew her targets shortly after making contact with them. Before Akari, she had never gotten to know her marks for long.

Thus, Momo wasn't wholly caught by surprise upon discovering what might lead to Menou's death.

"Darling...is far too kind."

"Mm-hmm." Akari nodded. "She's been that way since I first met her. Menou's really nice, at least to me... Hee-hee!"

"If only she could just abandon a nitwit like yooou...!"

As Akari giggled, Momo ground her teeth, wondering why Menou would risk everything to protect this awful person.

Menou's betraying the Faust meant she would be killed by her Master, Flare. And if that was a real possibility, Momo decided there was no need for her darling to kill Akari at all. She simply took Akari away from Menou so the Human Error wouldn't inspire her to do something foolish.

Momo had shifted her goal from a journey to take Akari's life to one to save Menou's instead.

"But, Momo, is Menou really going to be okay without us?"

If Menou and Akari's closeness was what triggered the disaster, then Menou would survive so long as Akari stayed away. However, Akari stayed with the priestess, reasoning that there was no guarantee that Flare was the one who would actually take Menou's life.

Akari had tried never meeting Menou at all, yet it resulted in her dying even sooner.

Momo rolled her eyes to express that Akari's concerns were pointless.

"She'll be fine. Listen, you may not have realized this because of how painfully stupid you are..."

"Momo, could you maybe zip your lips instead of insulting me again?"

"You may not have realized because you're so dense..."

Momo completely ignored Akari's pouty request, instead emphasizing the other girl's idiocy as she continued.

"But from what you've told me, it seems like there are two main causes for my darling's death. One, she's killed by the red-haired priestess you mentioned—Master Flare. This happens when my darling rebels against the Faust. And two... When you're not around, she doesn't have the strength to survive certain dangerous fights. I imagine this is primarily when she gets captured by Archbishop Orwell in Grisarika Kingdom."

This became clear when Akari decided to avoid meeting Menou.

Archbishop Orwell—a member of the Faust who stained her hands with extreme taboo. She was a powerful opponent. Individually, she far outclassed Menou, and she also strategically kept on the mask of a clergy member.

Menou had only survived her stronghold in the old capital of Garm because she'd managed to draw out Akari's Pure Concept. Orwell was so powerful that even Menou couldn't defeat her with an ace-in-the-hole source of strength.

Since Momo had assisted in that investigation, she was all too aware that Akari's absence would have made it impossible for Menou to defeat Orwell.

"Since there were two ways for my darling to die, you chose to try to save her by traveling with her, correct?"

"Yeah."

Akari nodded again.

Without Akari, Menou wouldn't have escaped Orwell's trap. This was essentially a confirmed fact. No matter how capable Menou was, she was poor sport for an enemy who stood at the top of the Faust.

"This time around, we've already overcome that trial. So what we need to worry about now is the possibility of my darling being killed by our teacher after crossing the center of the continent."

In other words, around when she left the Balar Desert: the events that were happening even as they spoke.

Akari had explained the loop during their time in the oasis to Momo. On their journeys since then, Momo had learned virtually everything else that Akari remembered.

From her understanding, things differed from the situation with Orwell when they entered the western part of the continent. Master Flare only killed Menou when she had spent more than a certain amount of time with Akari.

"But most likely, my darling…"

Momo trailed off. She didn't want to voice why Menou would betray the Faust, especially in front of Akari. She could imagine the other girl getting a big head about it all too quickly. If Momo spoke it aloud, she was going to regret it. Yet she reluctantly opened her mouth anyway.

"…I imagine her friendship with you will rob her of her will to take your life."

As far as Momo could tell, Menou died to Master Flare when she betrayed the Faust to save Akari.

No sooner did the assistant Executioner admit as much than a shameless grin spread across Akari's face.

"Oh yeah? Heh-heh… You think so, too? Really? I knew it! Menou must really, *really* like m—"

"It's all your fault, so diiiie!"

"Bwuh?!"

Her reaction was even more annoying than Momo had expected.

Momo swung a right hook at Akari as if to punish her for the sin of getting too full of herself. It was a very exaggerated, obvious move, so Akari quickly slid out of her seat and narrowly avoided Momo's fist colliding with her face.

"That was close! What the heck was that for?!"

"Ooh, I'm sooo sorry. You just got so ridiculously happy despite being the root of the problem, and I couldn't control my desire to destroy yooou."

"You're just jealous! Don't be mad just 'cause Menou obviously cares about me more than you!"

"Excuuuuse meee?! Aaas ifffff! Who do you think you aaaare?!"

Momo glared at Akari but lowered her fist. Even if she punched the other girl's head in, *Regression* would just bring her back. It wouldn't be fatal.

"Well, I certainly have a lot of doubts. But that hypothesis will do for now."

Among the most immediate of the many oddities that stuck out to Momo was that Master Flare, who was supposedly going to kill Menou, was not a currently active Executioner.

Flare was known as a living legend, but at present, her role was to supervise a monastery that trained future Executioners. Revered though she was, the woman would typically never be sent out into the field in her position.

Why would their Master come out of her retirement from the front lines, even to execute Menou for treason?

Menou was incredibly skilled, but she wasn't so strong that no one but their Master could possibly kill her. Even Momo's biased judgment had to concede that a squad of sufficiently skilled priestesses from the holy land could most likely defeat Menou.

While Flare had made Menou her successor, she wasn't such a sentimental person that she would insist on being the one to take her old pupil out.

Coldhearted and ruthless.

An emotionless killer.

Such was Momo's impression of their Master. Flare never let any feelings affect her mission. She didn't even place that much value on her own life. So why would she do something like this?

However, based on what Akari described from her multiple encounters with their Master, it was no coincidence. During the first time in particular, there was no doubt that Menou had betrayed the Faust to save Akari.

They didn't have enough pieces to put the puzzle together, though. So Momo set aside the pointless speculation and moved on to the next subject.

"So the biggest difference between this time and all the others is Pandæmonium, right?"

"Yeah, for sure. That was a shocker."

Pandæmonium was the Human Error they had encountered in the port city of Libelle. Known as the worst and most horrifying of the Human Errors, she had been sealed away in a fog, until a hole unexpectedly formed in the barrier. It was thought to be caused by a thousand years of deterioration, but as it turned out, Akari's repeated *Regression* of the time line was the real cause.

Momo couldn't help but scowl at this.

"Really, what a horrible thing to cause for all of us. Are you trying to destroy the world indirectly?"

"No, I didn't mean to…"

Akari pouted, clearly unhappy with the situation.

She genuinely hadn't known that her conjurings could potentially release one of the Four Major Human Errors.

"Although, I mean… If Menou's going to die anyway, who cares if the world gets destroyed?" Akari said.

"I know what you mean," Momo agreed with a perfectly serious expression.

Menou was that much more dear to both of them than anything else.

"I can't blame you for being willing to annihilate the world to save my darling. But if you put her in danger in the process, then that's another story. I don't care what Pandæmonium does when my darling's not around, but what if they end up in the same place?"

"Argh, you're right…!"

The pair of Menou-loving extremists carried on their discussion without caring for any other casualties.

"At any rate, there are several ways to ensure my darling's safety. First and foremost is your death. If an Otherworlder like you dies, it's not like you have any family who will complain. And the sooner you perish, the faster my darling's reason for betraying the Faust will disappear. Unfortunately, we'll still be left with Pandæmonium's pinky finger, but that isn't so bad assuming there will be no other damage."

"…Listen, Momo." Akari looked grave as she regarded the other girl's blunt observation. "I hate you, so I don't want you to be the one to kill me. If you ask me, there's a level of trust required to forfeit your life to another."

"What in the world are you saying?"

It was indeed a bizarre sense of values.

Clearly, this girl had gone completely mad in the process of rewinding time over and over. Momo looked at her with an expression bordering on pity for a pathetic fool.

"I can't kill you anyway, which renders this plan moot."

"Why exactly can't you do it, by the way? Even you should be able to end me with the Sword of Salt, right?"

"I'm afraid I wouldn't be able to get permission to use it. From what I'm told, you need to pass through the holy land to reach where the Sword of Salt is kept. Since I'm an assistant on the run my own superior at the moment, going to the holy land would be akin to surrendering myself."

"Oooh, I see." Akari nodded thoughtfully. "So you really can't kill me, then. I'm kinda relieved."

"If I could, I would have done it already... Meddling little pest."

"Oh-ho-hooo? Well, since you *can't*, I guess that just makes you some really cheap pesticide, huh? Sticks and stones may break my bones, but at least Momo can't hurt me!"

It was true that Momo possessed no means of slaying Akari. If the lost lamb died by any standard means, the Pure Concept of *Time* would bring her back.

"At any rate, we're agreed that the reason for my darling's death is different from the first part of the journey to the middle stages and beyond, correct?"

"Correct."

"Good. Then once she's crossed the Balar Desert, my darling won't get caught up in any incidents she can't deal with, even without you there. So please get that idea through your thick skull already."

"...Gotcha."

Under normal circumstances, Menou shouldn't encounter severe trouble like the archbishop resorting to taboo too often.

"You've never once tested to see if you could leave her side at some point without her dying?"

"...I was scared, okay?" Akari's voice quivered. "I think it was the third time around...when Menou died while I was gone. So I thought it'd be better if I stayed with her forever to make sure she didn't die."

That was the main reason Akari never left Menou's side.

The person she was trying to save had perished in some totally unrelated event, nowhere near her, and it wounded Akari deeply.

"Even if Menou dies, I can turn back time. Start over again. But if I don't even know that she's dead, I can't rewind time. Not knowing what's happening to her is unbearable."

After repeating things a few times, Akari had once tried escaping from the castle in Grisarika as soon as she was rescued—making it so she never met Menou at all.

Ultimately, she had wandered aimlessly on her own until she was caught by Flare and learned of Menou's death. Until then, she had assumed Menou was alive, and she hadn't been able to use the conjuring that rewound time for the entire world.

Akari was always far more emotional than logical by nature.

Her obsessive desire to be with Menou made it impossible to analyze the situation objectively.

Momo crossed her arms as she listened to Akari's confession.

Much to her own annoyance, she understood exactly how the other girl felt. She couldn't help but sympathize with the sentiment of putting Menou's life above all else.

"Well, we've got a lot of work ahead of us. I hope you're prepared."

"I know, but still, Momo..." Akari sighed. "My heart's just not in it, traveling with you, I mean. There's no excitement about sharing things together, no thrill. A journey in another world should be fun, you know?"

"Excitement, hmm?"

Momo narrowed her eyes. If Akari had already lived through the same trip multiple times, she was undoubtedly used to it by now. Surely she was only complaining to pick a fight.

Momo wasn't one to turn down such an offer, however.

"Well, this is your first time coming to these mountains, isn't it?"

"Huh? Yeah, I guess so."

"I see. You've only ever taken the trains across flatlands before, I imagine. If my darling took you to the Sword of Salt, she would go by way of the holy land instead of taking a detour like this. In which case..."

Momo turned her attention to what lay beyond the window. Since the train had entered this mountainous region, the tracks had become more winding, slowing its overall speed. And since the two girls were passing by the peaks...Momo spotted exactly what she was hoping to.

"Five...four..."

The assistant Executioner began a countdown. Confused by the sudden turn of events, Akari watched with a puzzled expression.

"Three...two...one...zero."

Just as Momo finished, the train entered a tunnel.

Then the inside of the train filled with light.

The glow emitted by the Guiding engines filled the underpass and flooded in through the windows. Akari and Momo's car was no exception, of course. The Guiding Light poured in through the window Momo had opened.

Akari's eyes widened at the misty glow of the unnatural radiance. The locomotive exited the tunnel before too long, though.

The sunlight shone in and canceled out the faint glow of the Guiding Light.

"...Well?"

Since Akari was accustomed to traveling across plains, she'd never encountered a tunnel before. As the girl gaped in the aftermath of the wondrous sight, Momo looked at her with a straight face.

"Exciting enough for you?"

"...Hrmmph!"

Akari's mouth twisted up into a scowl. She puffed her cheeks and turned away, trying to hide her obvious emotions out of spite for Momo.

"Not at all!"

Momo grinned smugly.

She'd won this round.

*　　*　　*

Far behind Momo and Akari's scheduled train, another locomotive was running on the same track.

It had a total of ten cars, from the engine at the front to the observation car at the rear. Its wheels clacked against the tracks, pushing it ever forward. It must have looked far more powerful than any ordinary train to an outside observer.

Three luxurious sleeper cars were hitched to it. A pleasant aroma wafted through one compartment of the first sleeper car.

The interior couldn't have been more different from what Momo and Akari were riding in. This was no ordinary train that one could board simply by purchasing a single cheap ticket at the platform counter. Were it not for the scenery flying by the window beside the table, the inside could easily have been mistaken for a room in a first-class hotel.

The passenger in this particular chamber was even enjoying a decadent multicourse meal.

Usually, this food would only be served in the dining car adjacent to the kitchen car, but this person had instructed an attendant to bring the food to them, with the table entirely laid out for a restaurant-style dinner.

The one enjoying this extravagant service and cuisine was none other than Ashuna Grisarika. As she finished the seafood course and took a break, the next plate arrived.

"Here is the next dish, Your Highness."

"What's the main course?"

"A steak filet poele, I am told. Then there will be a rose champagne gelatin dessert, and, finally, black tea. Will that be acceptable?"

"Perfect. You know your stuff."

Nodding at the attendant's polite report, Ashuna stifled a snicker.

The person bringing her food was dressed in a butler's uniform. However, the wearer wasn't a man. The servant delivering Ashuna's meal was a woman young enough to be considered a girl.

Ashuna called to her again, mirth plain in her tone.

"You know, I'm surprised. As absurd as it may sound coming from the one who forced you to do this, you're actually pulling it off quite well."

"I certainly don't want to hear that from the party who put me up to this, but...yes, I have trained in anticipation of all kinds of situations, so I am confident I can carry out most tasks with relative ease."

"Waiting tables falls within the scope of your duties, then? Perhaps you truly are prepared to fit in just about anywhere."

Ashuna nodded thoughtfully, then pointed at the seat across from her with her fork. It was a rude gesture unbefitting a lady of her status, but she made it look perfectly acceptable with her absurdly high level of sheer confidence.

"Why don't you have a seat? You can give me someone to talk to while I'm eating."

"...I'm afraid I must decline. I still have duties to attend to."

The butler girl bluntly rejected the invitation and turned briskly on her heel. She had to go back and forth from the kitchen many times to deliver the needlessly elaborate multi-course meal. Ashuna's gaze on her back was decidedly teasing as she left the compartment and entered the hallway.

The interior design of a train car this resplendent extended to its halls. The floor was laid out with a soft carpet underfoot, while the ceiling was engraved with delicate patterns. Dried flowers decorated the walls and filled the air with a pleasant, gentle scent that paired well with other equally elegant decorations designed and arranged to soothe the soul.

In the otherwise empty corridor, the girl in the butler costume heaved a sigh and tugged resentfully at the hem of her tailored shirt.

"Borrowing money really is the worst."

For indeed, the girl being made to wear a butler's outfit and wait on Ashuna was none other than Menou, a proud member of the Faust.

The reason a priestess like Menou was playing dress-up and serving Ashuna dinner was quite simple: She was indebted to her.

Ashuna had handed her a butler's outfit with the borrowed *in*. Her condition for the loan was that Menou act as a servant.

"Having me become a butler temporarily is such an absurd condition for lending funds. Not that it's entirely unexpected for Her Highness Ashuna to do something ridiculous, but still…," Menou grumbled to herself as she headed for the kitchen car.

She was dressed as a girl in a butler's costume, not outright disguised as a man. The suit did nothing to hide her feminine curves—if anything, it was designed to accentuate them.

Incidentally, Sahara's reaction to Menou's present circumstance was downright horrible. She kept cackling and suggesting that Menou should just become a permanent employee of Ashuna's until Menou finally silenced her by shoving her scripture to the bottom of her luggage. She didn't intend to take it out again for some time.

©nilitsu

Sahara's bizarre situation still weighed heavily on Menou's mind. She couldn't help feeling like she was missing something important, despite not being able to put her finger on it.

"Is it because the Mechanical Society was involved? No… Perhaps because it was a conjuring that transforms the soul? Or is it something else…?"

Menou continued theorizing to herself as she made several more round trips through the empty hallway until the full-course meal was finally complete.

Ashuna wore a satisfied grin as she sipped on the black tea after her meal. She looked like a spoiled cat who was thoroughly accustomed to being waited on hand and foot.

"Who knew that having such an excellent butler could be this pleasant? I am utterly satisfied."

Menou, still dressed in servant's attire, poured Ashuna another cup of tea.

"I'm glad you're enjoying yourself."

"Indeed, I am."

Clearly, Ashuna really was relishing every moment. Menou didn't know anyone else who got such a deep enjoyment out of life. And yet Menou was so unlike Ashuna that she didn't feel the slightest bit of envy.

Instead, Menou was very uncomfortable on this train. There was a live performer on a grand piano in the dining car, for crying out loud. Riding first class on this luxurious train while not on an infiltration mission seemed wrong to her.

"At any rate, Your Highness. I should think it would suit you better to simply travel with a regular servant than have me pretend to be one, would it not?"

"The problem with regular servants is that they can only perform regular jobs."

"I'm not sure how such an obvious fact is an issue..."

"Can you blame me? I am fully aware of my habit of sticking my nose into danger wherever I go. It would be cruel to let a servant get dragged into battle because of my hobbies."

"...But you have no intent to restrain yourself and behave like a normal princess, I see."

"If I did, would I still be myself? Besides, I do not stand to gain anything by restraining my nature. I would much rather enjoy the journey my way." This was typically egotistical logic for the willful and self-conceited Ashuna. She inhaled the scent of her black tea before continuing. "In this particular case, I get to have you indebted to me, of course, but I'm also pleased to chase Momo."

Menou had been reluctant to let Ashuna join her. After all, she was in the middle of pursuing Momo. Bringing Ashuna along seemed like nothing if not a headache.

Yet since she was borrowing money from the woman, she was in no position to refuse. It was still better than pathetically losing Momo's trail because she didn't have the funds to keep up. Thus, she had elected to become Ashuna's attendant temporarily.

"Now, I've become your patron to cover the costs of finding Momo, but do you have any idea where she might be?"

"Of course I do. The actual act of following her won't be that difficult. Excuse me..." Menou paused and produced a map. "Once they leave the central desert, Momo's first stop will be the same town we're headed for."

"Hmm? How can you be sure? If we don't know Momo's intent, surely we lack enough information to determine where she might travel."

"No, I can predict most of Momo's moves."

Wandering around and searching blindly was a waste of time. The continent was enormous. Under usual circumstances, gathering information about the two runaways would require a significant amount of time.

However, Menou knew exactly how Momo's mind worked.

"Momo is undoubtedly traveling by train. We're currently following them in a locomotive on the same track... Fortunately, since this train is faster than ordinary ones, we should already be closing the distance."

"How do you know they aren't journeying on foot or by carriage? Then we might very well pass them."

"I seriously doubt it. A pair of girls trekking on foot would draw far too much attention, and Momo currently has someone slowing her down."

Momo was with Akari. She would never choose to go on foot knowing that Menou was tailing her. Compared to Menou and Momo, who had been trained as Executioners, Akari was far slower.

Most of all, two young women traveling together were bound to stand out. Momo might be able to roam without catching anyone's eye, but not with Akari in tow. Menou openly wore her priestess's robes while with Akari to make it clear to everyone around them that she was a member of the Faust, thus avoiding suspicion.

"I see. The girl I saw on the beach at the oasis, eh?"

Ashuna had probably guessed that Akari was an Other-worlder. She didn't press the matter further, but her eyes narrowed for a moment.

"But even if we know they're riding a train, how are we going to follow their trail? Guiding trains must follow tracks, but there are plenty of stops where they could disembark. The two could transfer to another line, as well. What do you plan to do about that?"

"I don't need to do anything. So long as I know their first hideout, I don't need to follow their trail any farther."

"Oh-ho?"

A note of delight entered Ashuna's tone, her interest piqued.

With a sidelong glance at her, Menou traced her finger across the map as she followed Momo's thought process.

"Momo can't keep moving for long with Akari in tow. Once she thinks she's bought herself enough distance, she'll choose a town with frequent traffic and hide out there. Momo is likely operating under the assumption that she's succeeded in slow-ing me down, so she won't choose a route that's too reckless. All of which narrows down where she'd choose to hole up for a few days."

Menou was familiar with the features of most of the major towns and cities on the continent. As she explained her logic, she pointed at one spot on the map.

"In which case, she will likely head to this mountain town first."

Ashuna clapped lightly, applauding Menou's detective work.

"Oh, you really are good. What do you think? I wouldn't mind taking you on as my attendant permanently."

"I'm honored by the invitation, but I'm afraid I must humbly decline."

Menou maintained the polite attitude of a servant as she calmly shot down the offer.

Ashuna grinned mischievously, unfazed by the girl's cool reply.

"Well, if anything ever changes your mind, the offer is always open. I'd be happy to have you. Especially since Momo would be bound to come along as well if I get my hands on you."

"The answer is still no, regardless."

Clearly, that was what Ashuna was really after, but it didn't change Menou's response. The position of a priestess was not so cheap that she would leave it for a small sum of borrowed funds, not to mention dragging Momo along with her.

"You seem quite fixated on Momo, Your Highness. May I ask the reason?"

"I wouldn't say I'm *fixated*, but...aside from her strength, of course, Momo is very entertaining to watch—and all the more so to tease."

"...She despises you because you mock her so much, you know."

"Are you giving me a word of advice as her 'darling'? It's equally amusing if she hates me, though. As long as she isn't indifferent about me, it means I stick in her mind."

Menou's comment didn't seem to have bothered Ashuna in the least. From her response, Menou had to wonder if the word *brazen* was invented solely to describe the Princess Knight. She pinched at her butler uniform, her lips turning downward.

"And is this ensemble a part of your 'teasing' as well?"

"Perhaps, but it is a precaution, too. I can't very well have you waiting on me dressed as you usually are. It could cause no small amount of trouble if people noticed that a priestess of the Faust was waiting on a member of the Noblesse like me."

"That logic makes sense in itself, but your particular choice of clothing baffles me."

"Well, there are only two options for a servant to wear: a butler's outfit or a maid's one. Out of those two, I thought the butler's would be more entertaining."

Her motivations were so openly selfish it was almost impressive.

Ashuna clearly looked amused as she looked Menou up and down. For her part, Menou had long since abandoned any semblance of a sensitive soul that would make her feel embarrassed by a mere change of attire, but she still didn't enjoy being toyed with.

"No matter, just think of it as a disguise. Although, I suppose I could have lent you something from my personal wardrobe..."

"I'll stick with the butler outfit, thank you very much."

Ashuna's garments wouldn't suit anyone but Ashuna herself. Menou was confident that she did not want to don anything in the princess's skimpy repertoire.

"Honestly. You really do get a lot of enjoyment out of life, don't you, Your Highness?"

"I wouldn't say that. Even this journey is just a way of staving off boredom."

"Oh?" Menou raised an eyebrow.

There was more emotion in Ashuna's voice than she had expected—or indeed than the princess herself likely intended to convey.

And so Menou found herself posing a question she hadn't meant to.

"Why did you leave the Grisarika Kingdom, Your Highness?"

"I am sure you know. I did not want to get involved in the scuffle over the line of succession following my father's death. That is the biggest reason."

"You had other reasons, too, then?"

Ashuna looked up, peering into Menou's face curiously.

"You're surprisingly inquisitive. What's gotten into you, hmm?"

"Revenge, I suppose. Since you forced me to wear these clothes, it seems my tongue is now more prone to slipping."

"I see." Ashuna chuckled at the barbed comment. "Well, to be frank, I hate my elder sister, you see."

Her admission brought a hush over the room.

Only the rumbling of the train filled the silence.

Despite her claim, there was no hatred in Ashuna's voice, nor anger, nor fear. If anything, the emotion seemed closest to sorrow. It was a "hate" filled with complex feelings, uncharacteristic of the normally straightforward princess.

"By your sister, you must mean..."

There was only one other girl in the Grisarika royal family besides Ashuna: the king's eldest daughter.

She possessed far less presence when compared to the widely famous Ashuna. Few people even knew her name. Menou did, but nothing else. From her point of view as an Executioner, the elder princess had no records that made her worth noting, for good or for ill.

"She was always sickly—a frail person. So much so that a passing breeze might knock her to the ground. She spends most of her day in bed and can't even walk without help. It's been that way ever since her birth."

What did that mean?

Ashuna's description seemed like it should inspire sympathy, not disgust. The other princess sounded like the polar opposite of Ashuna, but that didn't explain Ashuna's hatred. While the ostentatious Noblesse valued strength above all else, she didn't seem the type to despise the weak.

Perhaps it was the other way around, then?

"So did your elder sister detest you for being such a natural prodigy, then?"

"No, she adored me to a terrifying degree... Ah, I suppose that's one way to put it. In all the world, she's the only thing that scares me. I am terrified of her love."

Was her feeble elder sister using her position to persecute Ashuna somehow? The princess did not answer, content to shrug.

"If I had stayed there any longer, she would likely have used her influence to put me on the throne. Even if I went back now, she might still. To be honest, I don't want to return at all. But I will have to, one of these days." Ashuna's voice dripped with bitterness. "This journey is a way of killing time, but it is also an escape, a method of enjoying my final grace period. I still have no answer as to what I should actually do."

"That's surprising, given your penchant for snap decisions."

"Yes, that is part of the problem."

Although Ashuna appeared to live according to her whims, she still possessed a sense of responsibility. She was not liable to cast off her position.

"And if I may complain to you a little more, there's the matter of my father being executed over the Otherworlder summoning. That was a serious inconvenience to me, you know. Putting him in the firing line advanced the question of his successor significantly."

Akari had been brought to this world by the Otherworlder summoning incident in Grisarika Kingdom. If Menou recalled correctly, Ashuna had fled the royal castle immediately after.

"...Who *is* your sister, Your Highness?"

"Who can say? I thought you might know her, but it seems not." Ashuna paused to flash a grin. "I would be pleased if you found the answer somewhere on your trip."

"Is that right...?"

Feeling mocked again, Menou shook her head, and as the two continued to chat, the train rumbled on.

With Ashuna's help, Menou was on track to catch up to the others much sooner than Momo was expecting.

CHAPTER 2

The Escape Takes
a Rest

It had been about half a day since they'd crossed the desert at the center of the continent and boarded a train. When they arrived at Momo's chosen destination, Akari became strangely excited.

"Honestly! You are such a meanie, Momo."

Her voice a full octave higher than usual, Akari clapped Momo on the back, her insults lacking their usual bite.

"I mean, I knew you were a big jerk, you know? Obviously, I knew that. But this is just crossing the line! Really, why didn't you say so sooner?!"

"Is that right? You're one to talk, now that you've dropped the Goody Two-shoes act."

"But come on!" Akari gestured dramatically at the town they'd arrived in and raised her voice even louder. "You should've just told me we were going to a hot spring!"

She was practically bouncing up and down. Momo glared at her coldly as if to say that her excitement in itself was unbearably annoying, but a native Japanese person's love for hot springs, carved into their very DNA, wouldn't be cooled so easily.

"It's such a wonderful surprise that I almost like you a little more now!"

"If I thought it would make you like me more, I would have chosen someplace else."

Akari hummed a cheerful little tune, oblivious to Momo's unamused reply.

Since Momo had changed her usual route so drastically, this was Akari's first time coming to this town. In other words, out of all the many time loops Akari had experienced, she had never before seen the famous hot spring locale.

Momo's shoulders slumped in visible regret at having made Akari happy.

"I've made a serious miscalculation... Why would you get so excited about some stupid warm water coming out of the ground anyway?"

"Don't be ridiculous! Weren't you supposedly taught all about Japanese culture in your training as an Executioner?! You've got to know something this basic, geez!"

Akari was practically foaming at the mouth as she began extolling the virtues of hot springs.

After all, she had primarily been living life on the road since she came to this other world. Even a chance at a hot shower was a luxury as far as bathing went. Akari hadn't enjoyed a warm bath since the one she'd taken with Menou in the port town of Libelle.

"You're so disinterested because you don't know how wonderful hot springs are, Momo. Ah, the sheer bliss of soaking in steaming hot water...! And natural hot springs have even more benefits, like mental rejuvenation, clear skin, perpetual youth...

You can even boil an egg in them to make *onsen tamago*! Hot springs aren't just healthy; they're also delicious!"

"I'm sorry to interrupt when your brain is clearly being boiled, but we didn't come to this town to soak, you know."

"Huh?"

Akari's body, which was bouncing around in excitement, suddenly froze. Her eyes widened in shock, still sparkling at the thought of hot springs.

"Wh-what do you mean? Since we're here, we must relax with a nice, long bath to show our respect. Anything less would be an insult to hot springs everywhere... No, to the very gods who created them, who would be sure to punish us. The only thing to do in an *onsen* town besides taking a bath is to eat a tasty *onsen tamago*, you know?"

"No, I certainly do not. We're here to escape my darling and to train that useless lump you call a body while we're at it. I don't give a single damn about your dumb steaming pond."

"Train?"

While the hot springs were still bubbling up in Akari's brain, Momo dismissed her ideas as thoroughly worthless and explained her intentions for this stop. Evidently, rest was not on the menu.

"I had a lot of questions after hearing about your time loops, but I noticed something... No matter what time line, you've done very little fighting, right?"

"Huh? Well, yeah, I'm not really big on combat..."

"Hah. No wonder you're so absurdly weak despite having a Pure Concept."

Akari fell into a depressed silence.

Momo and Akari had clashed once before traveling together. Akari had possessed the element of surprise, yet she'd still struggled to gain the upper hand. Had they continued, Momo likely would've grown accustomed to Akari's conjurings and taken the advantage.

Akari's natural disposition simply wasn't inclined toward violence. On top of that, she had absolute faith that Menou would protect her if she got in trouble and the advantage that she wouldn't die thanks to her Pure Concept of *Time*. Frankly, she did not need to fight.

She couldn't die and had the option to start things over. These qualities had fostered an overly lax attitude that prevented Akari from getting any stronger.

"So that's why you're always dragging my darling down... To put it mildly, wouldn't we all be better off if you died?"

"...Why do you have to be so hurtful, Momo? If you've gotta say stuff like that, you could at least sugarcoat it."

"Because I hate you, and I want to make you feel bad."

Momo's tone was so light that it barely even sounded like an insult anymore. She loathed Akari, and Akari felt the same way toward Momo. This was an absolute truth, a mutual understanding between them.

Yet now Akari was giving Momo a genuinely wounded expression.

"I get it now. You're nasty to me because you despise me..."

"It's a little late for that, isn't it?"

"...which means, since Menou was always nice and sweet to me, she must really love me."

"Are you familiar with the term *customer service*?"

As Akari got carried away with a self-serving interpretation of reality, Momo grabbed her shoulder and dragged her back down to earth.

"When you're on the job, you have to be polite to everyone, no matter how foolish they are. My darling must have had a hard time dealing with you for the last two months, I'm sure."

"...Oh yeah? Then, since you're mean to me on the job, I guess you're still just an inexperienced child, huh, Momo?"

"...Yes, I suppose. I am still an assistant priestess, so I lack my darling's level of professional behavior. When I see an idiot, I can't help treating them like one...you idiot."

As had become typical, the pair was starting another verbal battle, each searching for the other's weak points to deal damage whenever possible. Neither stood to gain anything, but they kept polishing their techniques nonetheless, making any reconciliation between the duo all the more hopeless.

There was no point in continuing this unresolvable quarrel, so Akari reluctantly raised a different question to Momo.

"What exactly do you mean by training me?"

"It's simple. You just need to get accustomed to using your Pure Concept powers in combat. We should think about the most effective ways to do so, too."

Akari blinked in surprise at Momo's suggestion.

"But Menou told me never to use my Pure Concept unless I have to."

"It's a little late for that." Momo shot the other girl a droll look. "Pure Concepts carry the risk of turning into a Human Error, yet you already use yours all the time, don't you?"

"Well, yeah, I guess... But since I've already used it so much, doesn't that mean I shouldn't push my luck?"

"Well, about that. Your Pure Concept doesn't seem to erode

your mind nearly as quickly as it does for any Otherworlder I've heard of."

"Really?"

"Yes, really. It's a very dramatic difference compared to any example I know. Maybe it's because your mind is already so dense that it's hard to damage?"

When Otherworlders used their Pure Concept powers, they consumed their own memories.

For instance, the *Null* boy who'd been summoned along with Akari was affected so drastically by a single use of his Pure Concept that it changed his entire personality. But Akari, who was constantly employing conjurings on a global scale but hadn't turned into a Human Error yet, still possessed a firm grip on herself.

"Pure Concepts create conjurings far more powerful than any other kind. Please learn to use it in battle as well. If you get proper command of your Pure Concept, most humans won't stand a chance against you."

"Yeah, maybe... But you know my conjurings aren't free, right? They erase my memories."

"Well, we have a simple point of reference for that. Your recollection of your world, of Japan, should disappear first. By rough estimation, as long as you haven't forgotten Japan entirely, you should still be fine, and your memories with my darling won't disappear."

"Mmn, I guess so... Are you sure you're not up to something, Momo?"

"Hmmm?"

Akari was very reluctant to use her powers more than

necessary, especially after Menou had repeatedly warned her against it. As she hesitated, Momo glared at her with utter contempt.

"I'm proposing this for my darling's sake, yet you refuse even to try. If your memories from the other world are more important to you than my darling, I guess that's fiiine? Maybe your attachment to her wasn't quiiite as strong as I thought."

"Ex*cuse* me?"

Something snapped, and rage burned in Akari's eyes.

"I don't know what you mean, Momo. My feelings for Menou are about a hundred times stronger than you realize, just so you know."

"Go ahead and prove it, then. Listen closely, you useless girl! If you bothered to train a little, you'd be able to save my darling someday instead of just letting her rescue you all the time!"

"Fine! I'll do it, just you watch!"

The Menou-shaped bait worked perfectly. Immediately, Akari's motivation shot through the roof.

✳✳✳

The scent of sulfur was strong in the mountain town's air.

It was famous for its natural hot springs, and wooden inns, restaurants, and other attractions lined the streets. A train station served as a spot on a line connecting several major cities, which helped the town prosper as a tourist area.

There was an outpost for the knights of the Noblesse, who were in charge of keeping order in the area, and a small church to indicate the presence of the Faust. Otherwise, it was populated with Commons citizens.

As a combination health resort and sightseeing locale, the settlement enjoyed a steady torrent of visitors. This also meant it sometimes provided a hideout for criminals and taboo perpetrators who needed to avoid attention.

The man known as the Recruiter was one such criminal.

Occasionally, those who worked in shady businesses had a falling out with a group. Some might botch a job and find themselves banished, while others might have fled and lost a place to call home. The Recruiter's objective was to gather these pariahs and find them suitable jobs.

The man called the Recruiter initially belonged to an ideological group known as the Fourth.

All citizens of this continent were separated into three castes: the Faust, the Noblesse, and the Commons. These strata and their rules were the foundation of the world order.

The Fourth lit flames of discontentment with the caste system that had existed for so long.

They agitated the dissatisfied Commons, fanned the inferiority complex of the Noblesse, and once assembled many to take on the Faust.

For a time, the Fourth grew so explosively that they even threatened to take over the Faust's holy land, but their activities died down when their leader, the Director, was captured. As a result, many skilled members of the Fourth were left without any employment prospects.

It was then that one man took on the duty of harboring the people of the Fourth, and he made a profit by charging a fee for offering temp workers. He started a hot spring inn as a cover that ended up becoming a legitimate business, but his primary profession was still as the Recruiter.

The present era was challenging for former Fourth members. He endured quietly without revealing himself until one day, when his patience was rewarded with good news that seemed to clear up the fog.

The Director, the founder of the Fourth, had been freed.

He had been detained in Grisarika Kingdom, a major power in the east. After stirring up chaos on the continent, he'd been sentenced to execution. His release could never have been official. Word was spreading like wildfire that someone had helped him escape.

However, the Recruiter remained skeptical about whether the Director had truly been freed. The information was far too perfectly timed for the Fourth.

Of the nations scattered across the continent, Grisarika Kingdom was particularly infamous. Recently, their archbishop, Orwell, was discovered engaging in taboo and was formally put to death as a result. Not wanting to get his hopes up prematurely, the Recruiter was cautiously gathering information.

A request to visit from the Director himself.

The messenger who delivered this news was a young girl in a kimono.

She wore her dark-indigo-tinted hair in a long braid. Speaking in an unhurried drawl, she informed the man that the Director was safe and would soon make a personal visit.

Tears of joy streamed down the Recruiter's face. Now the restoration of the Fourth could begin. He was wholeheartedly preparing to welcome the Director...

And then a priestess in white robes arrived in town with a black-haired girl in tow.

Having worked in the underworld for so many years, the man was immediately suspicious.

It would be far too optimistic to assume that they were here for nothing more than tourism. It was far too conspicuous to be a coincidence. Members of the Faust, who practiced honorable poverty, were unlikely to indulge in a frivolous sightseeing trip unless it was part of a pilgrimage.

No, they had to be there for the Director.

The man could not simply turn a blind eye. Using his connections as the Recruiter, he gathered up a few combatants and issued an order:

Dispose of the priestess girl who'd come to investigate.

Upon receiving the order, the fighters quickly formed a plan.

They were active in the field and very familiar with all kinds of dishonest work. Some were adventurers who had fallen to more shadowy endeavors, while others were researchers who had been driven to the darkness by their thirst for knowledge. But one thing they all had in common was that they'd long since abandoned any pretense of decency that would make them hesitate to kill young women—especially if one of them was a priestess.

There was no need to challenge her head-on. They had the home field advantage, so waiting for a moment when her guard dropped was preferable. Since the target had entered a hot spring inn, striking while she was bathing seemed perfect.

Sure enough, the black-haired girl traveling with the priestess was gleefully exclaiming "Hot spring! Hot spring!" During check-in, her attitude toward the priestess had been sullen at best, but now she was obviously in high spirits at the prospect of a warm bath.

The priestess had a small frame and childish features. She couldn't have been more than fourteen years old. Her wearing priestess robes instead of a nun's habit despite her youth meant it was safe to assume she was a natural prodigy. But since the robes were white, it was clear that she still had a ways to go.

The fighters smirked. This was going to be easy.

One of them, who was working as an inn employee, suggested that the two girls try the open-air bath during the afternoon. It was outside of normal operating hours, but the suggestion was meant to ensure that the pair would be alone.

Once the young women followed this recommendation and entered the bath, an armed man entered the changing room.

Priestesses were skilled practitioners of conjurings, but they had to use a vessel to invoke them.

Be it a crest conjuring or a scripture conjuring, these techniques were based in materialogy and crestology. Guiding Force was a great power drawn from the soul, but it wasn't easy to produce its full effects without the tools to control it properly. The mightier the conjuring, the larger and more complex the medium required.

Guiding Enhancement was an exception that could be invoked with only one's body, but the man was capable of that much himself.

Humans with weapons were inevitably stronger than those without.

No matter how skilled a conjurer this priestess was, she would be at a disadvantage when stark naked.

This went without saying, but the assailant still felt the need to spell it out because he was breaking into a women's bath.

What's more, the priestess was a presumed teenager. The shock and embarrassment of being attacked in the bath were bound to slow her reaction. The man estimated that he would defeat her before she could launch a counterattack.

Having entered the changing room armed with a weapon and this flawless logic, the man called his target's face to mind. The black-haired girl clearly couldn't fight, though it was a mystery why she was accompanying the priestess. The best approach would be to take her hostage to threaten the priestess.

As the man thought over his battle plan, he decided it would be best to ensure that the priestess couldn't recover her weapons no matter what, and so he took the girls' clothes out of their dressing room cubby.

Just then, the door that led to the open-air bath slammed open.

"Whyyyy do I have to take a bath with yooou instead of my dear darling?"

"Cut it out. You're going to ruin a perfectly good hot spring if you keep—"

They must have entered the bathing area, realized they'd forgotten something, and returned to get it. As the black-haired girl stood there with steam rising from her skin, she locked eyes with the assailant who had infiltrated the women's changing room.

"......"

"......"

There was an almost painful silence.

The black-haired girl was wrapped in a towel from the chest down.

Her bare limbs were sleek and smooth. The fabric could barely conceal her ample chest as it absorbed a small amount of perspiration from her cleavage. A single drop of water slid down the curved line of her thigh.

A faint *plip* sounded as the bead of liquid struck the ground.

The man regained his senses with a start.

His mind had gone blank at the unexpected development for only a moment. This was a warrior who had gone to tread the line between life and death countless times. His skills were not so meager that he would be deterred by the sudden appearance of a lovely young woman. He hadn't anticipated his target would come back into the dressing room, but perhaps this was the perfect opportunity.

If he took the black-haired girl as a hostage, it would be far easier to capture the priestess who was still in the bath. The man stepped forward to seize the girl.

"P..."

The girl's eyes clouded with embarrassment and burned with rage.

She aimed her index finger at the assailant like one might with a gun. As the man watched in bewilderment at her strange attempt at a threat, Guiding Light gathered in her outstretched fingertip and formed a conjuring.

Cold astonishment washed over the man. How was she invoking a conjuring without any Guiding vessel? What's more, this was a conjuring construction he had never seen before. His mind struggled to comprehend what was happening before him, rendering his physical response a moment too late.

©nilitsu

"Panty thieeeef!"

As the black-haired young woman shrieked, an unusually powerful conjuring lanced forth from her finger.

One of the would-be assailants was taken away by knights.

His attempted surprise attack in the open-air bath had failed. One of the targets had caught him in the changing room and managed to stop him somehow. Ultimately, he was arrested by knights under suspicion of stealing underwear.

The men the Recruiter had gathered were all part of the Fourth. They had undergone rigorous training to fight the priestesses of the privileged class someday. It was painful to have one of their fellows treated as an unsavory criminal, but at least it meant their marks remained ignorant of their true intentions.

It was better that the girls believed they had stopped a simple sex offender in the act than to have them suspect their lives were in danger. To keep the targets' guards down, their captured comrade had swallowed his pride and bravely declared "I am indeed a panty thief" when the knights hauled him off.

As for the girls who had reduced a proud warrior to a common pervert, they were now strolling around the hot spring town together.

The pair wore matching *yukata* as they walked, perhaps intending to take a full-on hot springs tour. One of the assassins who was blending in as part of the staff had suggested that they wear the rented garments, citing it as part of the fun of a hot spring town.

"This place has super-Japanese vibes, especially with these *yukata*. The rooms at the inn all have tatami mats, and the buildings are wood. The whole village is so rustic... It's almost shockingly similar to an old-fashioned Japanese settlement. This might be the first time I've been to such a familiar-looking locale. In a way, you could even say it's more Japanese than modern Japan."

"Mm-hmm. So this is what you'd call Japanese? Perhaps the local culture was strongly influenced by some lost lambs. There are mountains all around us, right? Until the train station was built, their community must have been isolated for a long time. People claim this town is surprisingly rich with history and ancient customs. The buildings may even be remains from ancient times."

"All Japanese people love hot springs, y'know. And some are extra enthusiastic about 'em, so I wouldn't be surprised if a person like that had a hand in this village."

"Perhaps this entire street is a remnant of the ancient civilization, then."

The two girls absentmindedly chatted as they walked.

They had easily dodged one dangerous encounter in the open-air bath at the inn, but there were still more perils surrounding them.

The first surprise attack had failed. It had been unwise to attack the young women alone, even if the attacker hoped to catch them when their guards were down. Thus, the next ambush was based on strength in numbers.

An attack on the main road would draw too much attention. So the group of assailants sent in a consort who worked in the area. The young man, a well-known lecher, was told to entice the girls and lead them into an unwatched alley.

The young fellow approached the pair, his pleasant air and

attractive features on full display. Nearly ten skilled assassins were waiting in the narrow street where he was to guide them. Even if she was unusually capable, that had to be more than enough to dispose of a single priestess.

"Hello, ladies—"

"Die."

"Die?!"

The handsome man couldn't hide his surprise at the immediate rejection.

It was the priestess girl who'd replied so bluntly that it was painfully obvious she had no intention of continuing the conversation. She made an openly disgusted face, tossing her pink pigtails over her shoulder.

"Yes, just hurry up and die, please. I have no interest in small fries like you. Your very existence irritates me. Begone with you, and tell them to send someone a little more worth the trouble of defeating next time."

The young man, who believed he generally had a way with women, had to fight to keep his face from twitching at such an unexpected insult. What kind of twisted society would cause a young girl to earnestly wish another person's death simply because he spoke to her?

The consort swallowed the urge to reply that he wouldn't be talking to such an immature brat if he wasn't getting paid to do so.

Meanwhile, the black-haired girl looked on pityingly.

"Come on, Momo. Telling him to die is a little bit extreme…"

"I-it really is! Ah-ha-ha, your sense of humor sure is—"

"At least keep it to a nice *Go away, you creep.*"

"Oof…!"

The handsome man thought the black-haired girl was siding with him, but it turned out to be an ingenious trap. The word *creep* was a severe blow to his relatively high confidence in matters with women. Still, a man who made his living as an escort wouldn't let a slight injury to his pride crush his spirits completely.

Rejection was second nature to a pickup artist. It was perfectly normal to be ignored at first. Trial and error were all part of the process.

Still, in this particular case, he'd been hired to get results. The amount of money offered was enough to make him reluctant to back down easily.

He hadn't failed yet. The young man gathered his inner strength.

The pink-haired girl already looked irritated that he seemed intent on speaking to them again, but then her face brightened, as if she'd hit upon an idea. The handsome consort waited to see if she might offer up a topic of conversation and was surprised when she pushed the black-haired girl forward.

"If you're trying to pick us up, then here, you can have this healthy specimen. I can't think of a single use for her, so feel free to go off somewhere together and do whatever you like."

"Momo?!" the black-haired girl shrieked in surprise.

Even the veteran consort had never experienced a woman blatantly selling off her friend to him before. He had no idea how to react.

The girl being offered was equally brazen. No sooner had she realized that her companion was betraying her than she pursed her lips and glared sharply at the pink-haired young woman.

"Just because you're tiny, flat, and unlikable doesn't mean you should jump right to that. For all we know, this guy might be into that! In fact, he's gotta be, or he wouldn't have started with you. Hey, mister! If you have any pride as a pedo, you'll take this girl instead!"

The sudden accusation made the consort's face go dead serious; he happened to prefer older women.

"I am not a pedo."

"Come on, no need to be shy!"

He should never have taken this job.

As the man silently cursed himself for suffering the accusation without denial, each girl kept trying to give the other away. Thankfully, he somehow managed to get them to follow him to the alley, though it required an unbelievable amount of effort.

As soon as they arrived at the dead-end backstreet, the ten-odd men appeared and blocked the exit.

"Yesss, just in time—"

A fist smashed into the consort's face, cutting his words short.

"I told you to die, remember?"

Since they were out of view, Momo immediately opted to use violence. Her first victim was the handsome man who had led them to the alley. First, she struck him squarely on the nose. She grabbed his sleeve and threw him to the ground as he staggered back. Then, just as the wind was knocked out of him when he hit the ground, Momo mercilessly and repeatedly stomped on his face.

The man groaned in agony a few times, but even that soon stopped. The priestess looked down coldly at the unconscious body and said, "...Now my shoes are dirty."

After ruining another person's face, that was all she had to offer.

The damage to his handsome features was bound to harm his future as a consort.

Momo kicked him off to the side of the alley with alarmingly practiced ease, then looked around slowly.

"I thought you were just a pickup artist, but...this isn't half bad."

As she spoke, the luminous glow of Guiding Force surrounded Momo's body.

A shiver of fear ran through the group of assailants.

Guiding Enhancement. A Guiding Force manipulation technique that raised the user's physical prowess.

Priestesses of the Faust were strong. By nature, they had to be adept enough at manipulating Guiding Force to operate the complex Guiding vessels known as scriptures. There were rumors that the path to being chosen as an official priestess was even more complicated, including combat training in the Wild Frontier.

The men in the alley were aware of this, for those who worked in the criminal underworld studied their mortal enemies.

But the amount of Guiding Force that the girl before them was using to enhance herself was visibly next-level. It was a sign that she had more combat power than the average priestess.

This was not good. Making a snap decision, the men attempted to flee. They had wisely concluded that their ambush based solely on overpowering their targets with numbers would not be enough.

Unfortunately, Momo was already behind them.

It had been a mistake to choose a dead-end alley to trap their target. As Momo moved nearer, she slammed her fist into the ground.

A dull crash echoed through the small street.

The tremor that ran through the ground left no room for doubting the petite girl's might—spiderweb-like cracks spread from the point of impact.

Guiding Enhancement alone shouldn't have been enough to produce this level of superhuman force. The men froze in shock at the show of superiority.

"If any of you try to run, I'll be happy to introduce you to my fist like I did to that piece of trash."

How could a teenage girl be so merciless? Why did her eyes not contain a single trace of compassion, a virtue supposedly touted by her church? And hadn't she just caused major collateral damage to a home, making her something of a criminal herself? The assailants had many questions, but most dared not to voice them.

"Wh-what do you mean, *if* we try to run?" one of the would-be attackers inquired cautiously. "What should we do, then?"

It was clear that their group of ten was no contest for Momo. Still, she made no move to torment the men. This had to mean that there was something she wanted.

If they complied, would she let them walk away? The man who had posed the question certainly hoped so.

"If you can attack that dimwit there and win, I'll let you go."

Akari, who hadn't been granted the kindness of having any

of this explained to her beforehand, stared at Momo in utter disbelief. Her gaze seemed to ask, *Are you all right in the head?*

"I told you to learn to use your powers in combat, didn't I? At first, I thought this was nothing more than a bad pickup attempt, but I'm pleased to see that there was more to it."

"...Wait, Momo, is this why you wanted to go out?"

"Of course. Strutting around unguarded was bound to attract some idiots."

The men twitched. Had their target seen through their plan of attack from the very beginning? It was inconceivable.

However, they still didn't understand what Momo wanted. They'd tried to launch a surprise attack, but one of their marks had commanded they go after her companion. No average person could understand the logic behind Momo's suggestion.

"Since the effects of your conjurings are so strange, it doesn't matter if you can't control them too precisely. Just try some things out in real combat."

"Umm... I'm not very good at regulating it yet, though..."

"It's fine. You only need to keep practicing. Even if you waste some Guiding Force, it will work out, probably."

"W-wait!"

It was a plan that obviously valued firepower and force over finesse. The men frantically tried to stop her.

"It's dangerous to misuse Guiding Force without the proper training! Especially if there's Guiding Force discharge?! That's not the kind of thing a noncombatant should try!"

He was right.

This was absolutely the most reasonable response. It was a basic precaution detailed in any manual on Guiding Enhancement or other techniques. Guiding Force was an energy produced by the soul. Conjurings were precise techniques that used that power.

There were plenty of exceptions, however.

"Really?"

"No need to listen to a criminal's opinion."

Momo, who had very little concern for Akari's well-being, gave an irresponsible go-ahead signal.

The men steeled themselves. This was a far cry from what they'd expected going in, but they had no other choice. Their only hope was to protect the black-haired girl being fooled by this vicious priestess and run like hell.

The Faust really were a nasty bunch. Full of righteous indignation, one of the men reached out to save Akari.

When he grabbed her arm, she automatically pulled back.

"Eek!"

Unlike the short scream that came from her mouth, the results were anything but small and cute.

For just a moment, Akari's entire body shone with Guiding Light, and then the man who'd seized her detected a strange conjuring he was unfamiliar with. A moment later, he soared into the air.

All eyes in the alley followed the man as he flew in a perfect parabola.

This was the result of Akari swinging her arm too swiftly to be visible to the human eye. She flung the man so hard that gravity did little to stop him from rocketing skyward.

Then he fell back down with a gruesomely loud *SPLAT*.

It was an extremely painful-sounding noise. Fortunately, the man didn't stay conscious long enough to suffer from the impact. He dropped too fast for any attempt to protect himself and could have easily struck his head and been killed instantly. He was fortunate enough to land in such a way that he simply fainted and rolled across the ground, however.

"Ohh..." The black-haired girl looked embarrassed. "S-sorry about that... I guess I didn't hold back my [Acceleration] enough...?"

Akari was one who apologized for her mistakes. That wasn't exactly helpful in this particular situation, but it was still better to say sorry than not.

"L-look, Momo. I really don't know how to moderate my powers. Is this truly okay? Aren't we kinda...committing a crime here? Like, I sorta feel like we're the bad guys right now."

"It's fine. There's no need to hold back. Aim for maximum output and maximum results at all times, please."

"Are you sure...?"

"Of course I am. All self-defense is legitimate, so it doesn't matter what you do to criminals."

Clearly, Momo had no concept of "overkill." Judging by the confidence with which she made this statement, it was evident that she genuinely didn't care what happened to the men.

"Still, the amount of power you produce really is something. I suppose that's inevitable with all the Guiding Force you have...but we have the perfect test subjects here. Just keep trying out whatever you like."

The men shuddered at being designated test subjects.

They were the ones who initially sprung an ambush, yet now they found themselves the lab rats of a vicious experiment.

A so-called holy woman who suggested violent experiments on humans was a disgrace to her kind. But no one here really

©nilitsu

thought of Momo as a holy woman anymore. The men realized she was still an assistant priestess despite being more powerful than any typical one because her mental state drastically lowered her rating.

To their own misfortune, they were wholly correct.

"H-hey, priestess! Don't you feel any guilt about what you're doing?!"

"Guilt, you say...?"

Momo repeated the man's accusation as if it was a completely foreign concept.

"Hmm? I don't quite understand. Why should I feel any remorse about cleaning up garbage? Guilt is a negative feeling when you've done something wrong, isn't it? My actions are justified, so I'm fine."

The men were at a loss for words in the face of such emotional detachment.

They had been trained to keep a level head, just as she had. Empathy only got in the way when one had to get their hands dirty or make cruel decisions. Thus, the assailants had deliberately trained their minds to be cold and inhuman when necessary.

Yet the girl in front of them was a different story entirely. She didn't hesitate to hurt someone. Some rare individuals derived pleasure from inflicting agony, but that didn't describe this girl accurately. She simply used any violent means she deemed necessary, with no emotional response either way. It wasn't that she was suppressing her human emotions; she was merely as merciless as a conjured soldier carrying out its orders.

Was this the result of being raised under the church's

indoctrination? The strangeness of it all struck fear into the men's hearts.

Normally, one felt reluctant to hurt another. Becoming an emotionless killing machine was impossible. This young woman must have been born different. The environment she'd been raised in had been utterly isolated.

"Now then, shall we get down to it?"

"Hrmm... Well, if it's for Menou's sake, I guess I have no choice."

As a storm of unstoppable violence rained down upon the men, they were profoundly and painfully reminded of just how cruel the Faust could be.

Nearly ten more would-be attackers were taken away by knights.

They were charged with attempted assault after a failed pickup attempt and deemed a foolish group that was thwarted by girls who were nowhere near adulthood.

They likely wouldn't have been arrested for a proposition alone, but the fact that they had attacked a priestess was a heavy crime. The knights did their duties with an almost unusual level of efficiency and sentenced the men to be punished, not wanting to incur the wrath of the Faust over something so trivial. The discipline was simply to be branded as would-be pickup artists. Although this was lighter than the sentence for kidnapping, it was painful for the seasoned warriors to be treated as common pests.

The Recruiter's only remaining assailant was the one undercover as an inn employee.

Thinking of his comrades being interrogated at the knights' station and lectured for trying to pick up young girls at their age, the incognito ruffian gritted his teeth.

He and his comrades were vanguards of the Fourth, warriors who fought for freedom. It was far too demeaning for them to be dismissed as idiots who gave in to lust. Better to suffer an honorable death on the battlefield than meet one's end being treated as a sex offender.

"I think your aggressive nature is rubbing off on me lately, Momo."

"You've always been a dangerous girl with an affinity for violence. Or don't you remember that you tried to surprise attack me first?"

"Hey, I was just being nice. I tried to do it without hurting you out of the goodness of my heart."

"That's a strange definition of *goodness*. Are you sure you're all right? Did you lose your common sense along with your memories?"

"I don't want to hear that from you of all people..."

As he worked at the inn, the man's murderous feelings toward the carefree girls grew ever stronger.

They had dragged his allies' names through the mud, yet they were clearly unbothered. The final assassin decided on a nighttime assault to reclaim honor for his fellow Fourth remnants.

There was no need for a complicated plan of attack. He was a genuine inn worker. Years of hard effort had earned him the trust of his colleagues, so he could move freely through the inn without drawing any suspicion.

He would enter their room while they slumbered and kill them in their sleep.

It was a simple plan—so much so that it was surely airtight.

Soon, night fell and brought sleep with it. With the Master inn key stolen from the office, the man silently entered the girls' room.

The two young women who had driven his comrades into shame and despair were resting peacefully in the faintly moon-lit room.

The priestess girl slept with the utmost propriety. Her blanket was drawn up to her shoulders, and she was breathing softly and steadily. There wasn't a hair out of place.

Meanwhile, the black-haired girl was the exact opposite. She had kicked off her blanket and tangled herself up in the sheets, clinging to her pillow with a bit of drool at her lips and murmuring "Heh-heh, Menou…" in her sleep.

It was a slovenly sight, to say the least. The obi holding her *yukata* closed had loosened in her sleep, revealing a great deal of pure-white skin that shone faintly in the moonlight. Under normal circumstances, it would've been lascivious enough to make one sweat.

Yet the assailant only felt infuriated to think that this sloppy fool and her friend had brought his comrades to ruin.

He reached out for the black-haired girl's throat. Using Guid-ing Enhancement, he could snap her neck and be done with it in a matter of seconds.

It's over for you. Now die.

With fervent anger, he began to close his hand around the sleeping girl's throat.

* * *

The next morning...

Akari woke up completely unharmed and exclaimed in indignation.

"Aaargh! What the heck is wrong with this inn, huh?!"

She was angry enough to forgo her usual reluctance to wake up because of the man who was frozen like a sculpture by her bedside.

"First a panty thief, then a bunch of pickup artist creeps, and now a guy sneaks into my room at night... How many sex pests can live in a single town anyway?! This is messed up!"

It was a rare occasion that Akari, normally a sleepyhead, snapped awake so quickly. Her cheeks were puffed up with rage at having to turn in a criminal first thing in the morning.

"A tourist town shouldn't be this unsafe!"

"Yes, very shocking."

Momo, who had more or less figured out the situation by now, answered absentmindedly with a yawn.

After being given another ne'er-do-well, the knights and other citizens alike all expressed their sympathies. "Oh dear, so many people targeting a pair of pretty young girls traveling alone!"

"Maybe you're giving off a pheromone that attracts criminals?" Momo suggested. "Even I've never been assaulted three times in one day, as I recall."

"You don't seriously think this is my fault, do you?"

"Well, I *do* think you're a troublemaker..."

Momo knew full well that the offenses were due to the Fourth. She even had information that this inn was managed by a shady businessman called the Recruiter.

That night, Momo's eyes had opened as soon as the man entered the room. She watched through half-closed lids to see if Akari would die at least once, but just as the man's hand was about to brush against her skin, the *Suspension* conjuring automatically activated, much to Momo's horror.

"I can hardly believe you made an automatic conjuring trap."

"Yep. Usually, I can get my powers to do whatever I want, more or less. That includes automatic traps or whatever."

If anyone touched Akari while she was sleeping, they would instantly find themselves on the receiving end of *Suspension*.

Incidentally, her main target was Momo. She used her Pure Concept to set unconscious defenses to punish the other girl just in case she tried anything while Akari was sleeping.

"Is that right...?"

Momo nodded with a carefully neutral expression, but internally she let herself grow warier of Akari. She had assumed from the girl's overall blithe attitude that she couldn't achieve more than simple conjurings on an enemy in front of her. That had been dead wrong, however. Conjurings that automatically activated under certain conditions usually required a great deal of preparation and forethought. If Akari could accomplish it without even trying, she was more dangerous than Momo had believed.

"And what if you had accidentally rolled over and touched *me* because of your poor sleeping habits, hmm?"

"...I—I would've dealt with it somehow. I can always just deactivate the conjuring," Akari replied, well aware of her sleeping habits. If anything, she might have even been hoping that her willful negligence would lead to such a development. She couldn't say as much aloud, of course.

"S-so what are we gonna do today?"

"Good question. I suppose for now…"

"For now?"

Momo shrugged.

"Shall we take a morning dip in the hot springs?"

The pair's hideout on the run was swiftly becoming a pleasant vacation.

CHAPTER 3

The Escape at
Its Height

Manon Libelle was visiting a mountain hot spring town famed as a popular spot for relaxation.

She wore an elegant white kimono, and her geta sandals clacked along on the cobblestones. Her sophisticated style fit in perfectly with the *yukata* and old-fashioned wooden buildings of the village.

A cherubic little girl in a simple dress strolled hand in hand with Manon. She gazed around the town with her eyes wide.

"Mm, mm, how strange. Something about this place feels familiar somehow."

"I know what you mean. It is certainly a tranquil, calming atmosphere."

Chatting closely with each other, the two girls looked like sisters who were several years apart. It would've been a heart-warming scene to anyone who didn't know their true nature.

"So what are we doing here?"

"I thought it might be nice to have a little rest."

"Mmm?"

This particular visit was intended as nothing more than a break, with no sinister plans behind it, much to the younger girl's confusion.

After their battle with Master Flare, they barely escaped with their lives. It had been worth working with Pandæmonium to create a huge catastrophe, for it had drawn out Flare.

"We finished most of our preparations and confirmed what we needed to know in the last city we visited. I thought we might relax for a bit."

The two had caused a pandemic using Gluttony, one of the Original Sin Concepts.

Part of the reason for such a massive undertaking was to test the full power of the little girl, who was really just a pinky finger.

Her real self controlled nearly limitless power. With her whole body, she would be strong enough to infect all the living things in this world with Original Sin Concepts.

But since this Pandæmonium was only a fraction of the whole, her might was far from inexhaustible.

At most, Manon's companion could spread the Original Sin Concept to approximately the population of a medium-sized city. Since the scale of her conjurings was directly linked to the number of victims she could produce, that was the upper limit of Pandæmonium's pinky finger's power.

She could taint an entire settlement with Original Sin and offer its inhabitants up as sacrifices.

Alternatively, she could summon one powerful monster created by her real body for a limited time.

The former was perfect for causing chaos, the latter for mass slaughter.

"Vacation, vacation…vacation? What is that exactly?"

"It's a good thing every once in a while. Taking time to rest and relax is very important."

They had figured out the limits of Pandæmonium's pinky finger, but as a result, they used up her entire stock of sacrifices that she needed to produce power. Thus, Manon decided they would rest up in this town and gather some sacrifices while they were at it.

Pandæmonium looked a little sulky at the thought of peaceful rest. Manon held on to her hand so they wouldn't get separated as they walked toward the inn she'd chosen. Out front, a bound man was being taken away by a group of knights.

What in the world had transpired? Manon observed the situation, listening carefully to her surroundings to gather information.

"I heard a man tried to steal underwear from a young lady at this inn…"

"A big group attempted to assault one of the guests in town…"

"Not only that, but one of the employees tried to sneak into a young woman's room at night…"

"The manager here really needs to discipline his employees…"

All the whispered rumors had decidedly unsettling contents.

"……"

Manon silently covered Pandæmonium's ears.

Pandæmonium looked up at the woman questioningly, but Manon just silently shook her head. She knew a child shouldn't have to hear such awful things. Whether a girl who'd existed for

©nilitsu

close to a thousand years could really be called a child was certainly questionable, but Manon had already decided to treat her as one in accordance with her appearance.

Still covering Pandæmonium's ears, Manon turned around slowly. There stood the man who had so fervently recommended this inn.

He appeared to be in his midfifties, and he was wearing a bowler hat and carrying a J-shaped cane. The expensive-looking tuxedo he was wearing gave him the impression of an out-of-place gentleman.

Manon was less than fond of the man, but she did trust his abilities. He was older and more experienced than her, and he had sowed chaos across the entire continent in the past; there was no doubt he was an outstanding individual.

"Excuse me, Mr. Director…"

The man called the Director, who was smiling warmly at Manon, twitched in response.

"I believe you told me that this place was the perfect resort for some peaceful relaxation."

"Y-yes, I did indeed."

"You said this inn was managed by an old friend of yours, as I recall. That it was inexpensive, safe, and comfortable."

"Ha, ha-ha-ha…"

The Director chuckled nervously. Manon smiled back at him a little too brightly.

Despite having sacrificed her entire family, traveled with the Pure Concept of *Evil* that could destroy the world, and had the ridiculous goal of trying to go to her mother's homeland in the other world, she was still an adolescent. Given what

Manon had just heard about this inn, she was hardly eager to stay in such a place, being a girl of a young age.

"So do you have anything to say for yourself?"

"...I'm terribly sorry! B-but listen, Miss Manon! I do have contacts at other inns, so you may put your heart at ease!"

"I'm afraid that doesn't reassure me in the least."

Manon maintained her polite grin while scolding the Director.

As Pandæmonium watched the exchange with an appropriately childlike expression of confusion, her ears still covered, she murmured to herself, "Mm-mm... He hasn't changed a bit since we first met, has he?"

✷✷✷

Manon and Pandæmonium first met the Director about a month ago.

Their first encounter had been in a tower standing in a remote region of the Grisarika Kingdom.

It was so remote that there were no roads to nearby towns, never mind a train station. One had to wonder how long the tower had been standing in such an inconvenient location—and for what purpose. Most people didn't even know it existed, but one cloudy, moonless night, a jet-black monster clung unnoticed to its peak.

A monster was a living creature that had been taken over by a Concept of Original Sin and driven mad to the point that its impulses overrode its survival instinct.

And yet this monster was bizarrely calm and quiet as two girls peered over its back.

"That was a half-decent adventure in the sky. Wasn't it, Manon?"

"Yes, quite a splendid experience."

Manon and Pandæmonium climbed down from the creature's back and into the tower. Manon had become linked to Pandæmonium in Libelle, and it was on her suggestion that they came to this spire where the Director was being kept.

"Shall we find Mr. Director's room, then?"

After easily infiltrating the structure, the pair began to work their way down through the seemingly empty interior. They checked the rooms on the top floor, then continued on until they finally reached the ground level without finding anyone.

After searching a bit more, they discovered stairs leading to the basement.

"We did it!"

"Yes!"

Pandæmonium high-fived Manon with her tiny hand. Then they went down the stairs and found what they sought.

The prison in the cellar was set up as an unbelievably comfortable living area.

Even royals of the Noblesse were not granted such luxury. Manon peered around the chamber, intrigued.

It was like a VIP room for welcoming aristocrat visitors. The fact that the man in the room was dressed to match it perfectly only emphasized the strangeness of the situation.

The gentlemanly fellow raised a hand from the other side of the prison bars, looking unsurprised by Manon's arrival.

"Hello there. You are Pandæmonium's new underling, are you not? Good evening to you."

How did he know about Manon when he was locked in a jail cell, albeit such a luxurious one? The man chuckled lightly and ducked his head, taking control of the conversation.

"I am the Director. Pleased to make your acquaintance... Although, I suppose we will not know each other for long."

"It's nice to meet you, Mr. Director. Er... So you have no intention of leaving this place, then?"

"Does it look like I wish to?"

It did not.

While this was an underground jail cell, there was no lock on the door. It would open at the slightest push. And as the girls had learned from their thorough exploration of the upper part of the tower, there were no guards stationed here. If he wished to leave, he could do so at any time.

This was Manon's first time here, but she could already tell.

He wasn't being kept in a jail cell. He was here of his own free will.

"I am told you had comrades who committed terrorist attacks in an attempt to free you. Yet you prefer to remain here?"

"Oh, them? Such pitiful creatures. Those who know nothing occasionally take such foolish actions. That is the tragedy of the ignorant." He shook his head. "And Miss Orwell's deeds in misusing those fools are even more deplorable. In the end, her transgressions led only to...this, hmm?"

The Director held up a newspaper lying on his desk. How had he acquired such a thing living in this isolated tower?

It was from the day of Orwell's funeral service.

"Look at this. A great holy woman has perished. She once subjugated a terrible dragonblight, yet she was laid low by the mere apprentice of Flare. Truly, age is a terrifying thing..."

"I'm not so sure I would describe the archbishop as a 'great' holy woman. She was executed because she committed a taboo."

"Ah… Young people."

The Director looked pityingly at Manon's blank expression.

To think that one so renowned as Archbishop Orwell could fade in just a few decades. People forgot about others so easily, even if they weren't Otherworlders whose memories were chipped away by Pure Concepts.

"Whether she committed a taboo or not, Miss Orwell's greatness is beyond any doubt. At the very least, I shall continue to sing her praises. She was a great holy woman, I tell you. She committed a taboo precisely because she was more faithful to the Lord's teachings than anyone else."

The Director's tone was bittersweet as he spoke of the late woman.

He was the first to propose the ideology of the Fourth and worked hard to dismantle the current caste system and change the world. As such, he had knowledge of many people.

"Miss Orwell became an archbishop, but she put aside her scripture in her later years. Do you know the reason, I wonder?"

"Put aside…her scripture? Why would she do such a thing?"

"Because she had no choice but to part with it. A scripture is the Lord's eyes, ears, and occasionally, mouth as well. And since Miss Orwell was pursuing an ideal Lord and devoted herself to the taboo of *Ivory*, she was forced to abandon the weapon she was most familiar with… Miss Orwell was more devoted to her faith than most, however, so perhaps she relinquished her scripture out of guilt."

"The scripture is connected to the Lord? No, more importantly… The way you phrased that makes it sound like the Lord is not just a concept, but something or someone who actually exists."

"Precisely. It is an absolute certainty that the protector of the world exists in the holy land, surrounded by the Elders, much to my frustration. I must credit this feeling to the Mechanical Society, too... Ah, truly, how irritating."

"I see...," Manon responded vaguely to the man's mysterious words. "And why are you telling me this?"

"You came all the way here in hopes of learning such things, did you not?"

That was true enough. Manon sought the Director because she wanted to hear his views.

Pandæmonium would happily answer any inquiries about the ways of the world, but her reasoning was always a bit too destructive. Most of all, Manon couldn't trust one-sided information from a single source to be entirely true.

That was why she'd decided to make contact with the Director, but he turned out to be even more intriguing than she expected.

"Yes, that's true." Manon tapped a finger to her chin and thought for a moment before continuing. "I came to ask you: What is conjuring, exactly?"

"A good query." The Director nodded, looking satisfied. "The fact that you would question such a thing means you are already drawing close to the truth of this world. Very well. Out of respect for how far you have come...and more importantly, as a reward for the achievements of the little creature next to you... I will be happy to answer your—"

"I've changed my mind," Manon interrupted.

"Hrmm?"

The Director regarded Manon quizzically.

The young woman clasped her hands together and smiled at herself.

"Your connections, your reputation, and all the knowledge you gathered during your time. Will you bequeath all that remains of the Fourth to me?"

"Ha-ha-ha. You shall have to content yourself with the minimum amount of information."

The Director rejected the proposal without a moment's hesitation.

"A youngster such as yourself ought to earn her own achievements and fame. There is no reason to give all that one has to another person for free, save for love. Unfortunately, you are too young for me to harbor romantic feelings for you, and I am not your father or the like."

"It's true that I am only a girl, just as you say." Manon knew where she stood and went on to describe what she could offer. "That is why I require your help. You have everything it is that I lack, and I am sure I can offer you whatever it is that you lost, too."

"...Indeed? Do you not realize that this world is beyond repair?"

"Oh, but it isn't." Manon shook her head calmly and gave Pandæmonium a loving pat. "There is something I must fix. Why else would a little girl like me be able to travel with this one here?"

"...Hrmm."

This exchange gave the Director a glimpse into what Manon wanted. It was enough to elicit no small amount of empathy from him.

"Is that right...? Yes, I see. Well then, Miss Manon..."

"What is it?"

"The truth is: I do have a single regret. If you can grant me my wish, then I suppose I shall come with you."

"I will be happy to oblige, if it is within my power."

The Director's ask was simple. He had failed to act upon his love long ago and remained single, and he did very slightly regret that.

And so it was with a serious expression that he offered up his request to the girl who was around the right age to be his daughter.

"Would you be willing to call me Papa from now on?"

"I see."

Upon hearing the Director's request, the young girl smiled and gave a courteous bow. Then she turned around without a second thought.

"A dangerous man like yourself would be better off staying here forever. Now, if you'll excuse me."

"B-but why?!"

The man immediately flew into a panic at Manon's change of heart. But she saw no benefit in responding to the Director's plea. Manon started to walk away, but Pandæmonium's small hand tugged on her sleeve.

"Mmm, Manon. That man seems very upset for some reason. We're really leaving him?"

"Yes, we are. Let's go, shall we? He's simply too strange. I apologize, since it was my suggestion to meet the Director in the first place... However, it's clear we shouldn't get involved any further."

"W-wait! Please, don't go!"

As Manon ushered Pandæmonium out of the room, the Director finally jumped out of his seat.

Hearing this, Manon reluctantly turned back with obvious displeasure. "What, you're planning on coming out on your own? Would you stay away from us, please?"

"No, I cannot! I swear, I shall do whatever you need!"

"Oh, dear... What's wrong with this man?"

Thus, the Director left his prison and followed after the frowning Manon.

***

Manon Libelle was the type of person who made decisions based on feelings over logic.

She didn't have an impulsive personality by any stretch of the imagination. Rarely had she ever lost her temper and shouted at someone, burst out sobbing in the face of a sad event, or indulged in any other display of powerful emotions. Since her childhood was so repressed, the waves of Manon's temperament were, if anything, quite calm and level.

However, Manon did base her priorities on personal preference.

Her choices were dependent on what she liked more, not what was more advantageous.

Since she'd fulfilled her wish of becoming a taboo in Libelle and gained her freedom, she turned her attention more toward satisfying her own whims. The reason she was traveling with Pandæmonium, too, was that she found the girl's proposal pleasing when she initially revived Manon.

Presently, there was only one thing on Manon's mind—taking a hot springs bath.

"...And so, you see, that is the situation at hand. The rash of so-called crimes was actually perpetrated by a violent priestess girl named Momo. Those men are not sex offenders at all. They were only attempting to ensure that they could safely welcome us. That girl is still on the loose, and at this rate..."

The Director was standing in front of Manon, prattling on while insisting that the inn he had chosen was perfectly safe—and that he hadn't made a poor choice at all. Or something along those lines.

Evidently, a series of misunderstandings had led to a group of Fourth members being misconstrued as perverts and arrested. But what sort of wild mix-up led to assassins being taken for lowly sex pests? Manon didn't quite follow, so she let the Director's lengthy explanation go in one ear and out the other.

Manon didn't have any particularly strong convictions. She preferred not to be bound by obligations like duty and responsibility. She had only freed the Director as an incidental outcome of their first meeting. His following her around was something of an annoyance.

The only companions Manon desired were cute girls, not weird old men.

As the young woman made this earnest wish deep in her heart, she picked up a small teapot and poured herself some tea. The pot was an exceptional little object that used a simple conjuring crest to boil water. To any who couldn't use conjurings, it was an ordinary teapot, however, which made it seem an odd inclusion at an inn.

Manon took a sip of the tea and sighed.

She and the others were in an Otherworld-style room of a level rarely seen elsewhere.

The hallway had beautiful wood-grained floors, and each chamber was laid out with tatami mats. The wooden building had a strict rule against wearing shoes in past the entryway, a rarity. And guests were provided with *yukata* instead of bathrobes after using the hot springs.

Manon's father, who was a member of the Noblesse, was an ardent admirer of Japanese culture because of Manon's Otherworlder mother. The kimonos that Manon wore daily were indeed conspicuous, yet they paled in comparison to this Japanese-style inn.

There was a total of three people in the room.

The Director, who was still talking; Manon, who was more or less ignoring him; and Pandæmonium, who was sprawled out on the tatami.

The visibly youngest of the trio was wearing her usual white dress, rolling around quite adorably on the floor. Then, on a whim, she suddenly hopped to her feet.

Her unexpected motion drew the gazes of both Manon and the Director.

Pandæmonium ignored their attention, staring up into space with a gleeful smile spreading across her face.

"Did something come up?"

"Uh-huh. A very interesting girl is nearby. I'm going to go mess with her a little."

This inexplicable behavior was nothing new for Pandæmonium. Manon realized she was looking in the direction of the town's train station. She hesitated briefly, wondering whether to try to stop the little girl.

Pandæmonium was the personification of the Pure Concept of *Evil*. However, in her current state, her power was severely limited.

Any use of her abilities required a corresponding sacrifice. Not long ago, she had spent nearly all her reserves in the battle against Master Flare. Pandæmonium only possessed about ten people's worth of sacrifices remaining at the moment. She was in no danger of dying, since she could offer herself as a sacrifice to summon a new copy of herself, but she was unreliable in battle.

"All right... Be careful."

"Mm. I'll be sure to bring back a souvenir."

Ultimately, Manon let the girl do as she wished.

Manon didn't really have genuine control over Pandæmonium anyway. Pandæmonium harbored no real intentions of her own. She acknowledged Manon because the *Evil* of the world had deemed her a necessary individual.

Someday, Pandæmonium would undoubtedly plunge Manon into the depths of hell.

As likely as not, she would consume the entirety of Manon's existence and forget about her, all while sporting the same innocent smile that she wore now.

And that was fine.

Manon Libelle was content to travel with Pandæmonium, knowing full well that such an end awaited her.

"You should come outside, too, Manon. I bet you'll have a wonderful chance encounter!"

Pandæmonium giggled cherubically as she left the inn to tempt someone to wickedness.

*   *   *

When she heard the train slowing, Sahara knew from her place within the scripture that they had safely arrived at the hot springs town.

At the moment, she couldn't see anything outside. Menou had shoved the scripture that contained her spirit deep into the bag she carried at her waist.

As she was hauled around like a piece of luggage, Sahara calculated that they were roughly two days behind Momo and Akari. That said, it made no difference to her whether Menou caught the girls.

No, that wasn't entirely true. When Menou reunited with Akari, she would take her to the holy land. When they got there, the priestess would hand over the scripture with Sahara still inside.

From there, Sahara's best outcome was being burned. If she was truly unlucky, they might experiment on her.

Either way, the day of her execution was drawing closer, and Sahara couldn't even move on her own. Thinking about the inevitable future gradually wore down Sahara's spirit. But she knew this was a punishment for her deeds.

As Sahara was sinking into a pessimistic spiral, Menou and her traveling companion disembarked from the train and parted ways.

Ashuna was sending Menou into town to check into the inn. The princess likely planned to unwind in the train station's rest area, then take her time heading over to the inn once their room was ready. She was clearly accustomed to putting other people to work on her travels.

Lucky her, Sahara thought bitterly.

They had never actually spoken a single word to each other, but Sahara deeply disliked Ashuna Grisarika. The princess's immense self-confidence was bothersome, and her overly familiar attitude rubbed Sahara the wrong way, too. Even if Sahara had been in a healthy state, she certainly wouldn't have wanted to befriend Ashuna.

So she kept her Guiding Force hidden, hoping the other girl wouldn't notice her.

Truthfully, Sahara wished to disappear entirely.

Being a nobody was intolerable. She struggled and suffered with bitterness and jealousy, and when she finally realized that her abilities would never reach the level of a person she longed to be, her life fell apart.

Envy.

This feeling was the basis of a conjuring counted among the Original Sin taboos, and it was Sahara's sin: the desire to become Menou that finally broke her.

If only her soul, her font of Guiding Force, would vanish. If only her spirit and thoughts would cease to be. If she was going to be killed anyway, perhaps she could just make herself disappear instead…

Or not. A wave of annoyance struck Sahara.

Why should she have to perish anyway? Since Sahara still existed, she decided she might as well inconvenience Menou as much as possible to the very end, remaining like a thorn in her memories.

As Sahara was forming these deeply negative new principles, Menou returned.

This was faster than Sahara expected. Evidently, Ashuna felt the same way.

"Hrm, that was fast. Were you able to get a room?"

"Yes. However, they said check-in would take some time and requested that we wait here a bit. Is that all right?"

"Oh? I suppose I'll enjoy your service for a while longer, then."

"As you wish, Your Highness."

Menou seemed to be getting quite accustomed to playing the part of a servant. She smiled sweetly, still clad in a butler's uniform, and headed over to the food counter to acquire some light snacks. From the look of it, she was ordering Ashuna's favorite black tea.

"Here you are."

"Excellent."

Menou brought the tea over to Ashuna, who accepted it with a haughty nod. She seemed to be enjoying playing the part of Menou's Master.

As Ashuna sipped the tea, Menou began gathering their things. As both were seasoned travelers, there wasn't much luggage between them. Menou didn't seem particularly invested as she sorted their belongings, and she carelessly touched Sahara's scripture.

"...?"

Sahara felt something strange.

In her current state, she didn't have the sensory systems of a human body. Sahara's soul and spirit were being fed information through the scripture's functions. And what it was currently collecting and sending to her contained something very unusual.

"......!"

When Sahara realized the source of the odd sensation, her soul trembled.

Even the moment before her death at Menou's hands hadn't shocked her this much. At the same time, she was relieved that her existence had miraculously gone unnoticed.

Sahara remained utterly silent until the person going through the bag finished putting her things back and moved away.

"That took a good deal longer than expected."

Checking into the inn was more involved than Menou had first believed. She grumbled to herself as she walked down the main road toward the station where Ashuna was waiting.

It was the Executioner's first time in this settlement. It took a while to find a fancy inn that might be to Ashuna's liking— and even longer to decide what level of room to get when she did choose an inn.

Ashuna wasn't likely to get upset over the wait, but she might very well tease Menou for it anyway. Feeling a bit glum as she neared the station, Menou was surprised to find Ashuna standing at the entrance.

"Hey, Menou. Done checking in?"

"Your Highness?"

Menou's eyes widened as the other girl greeted her with a wave. She hadn't expected the princess to come outside to wait for her.

The luxury sleeper train lived up to its name, after all. The ticket prices were accordingly exorbitant, but they came with far more services than any ordinary passenger received.

Holders of a luxury train ticket were granted various services anywhere on the train line. Naturally, that included within the train stations. Such passengers were allowed exclusive access to a special rest area in the station.

Menou had assumed that Ashuna would be relaxing in there, yet she had apparently come out to greet the priestess.

"Well, waiting inside turned out to be more boring than I thought. Here, you can take the luggage."

"Right… Thank you very much."

This was highly unusual for Ashuna. As Menou received the bags, she wondered why the princess was being so kind.

"Now, then. Let's see whether this hotel you took so long in choosing meets your standards, shall we?"

"Please don't…"

Clearly, Ashuna only came out because she was eager to resume her teasing. Menou sighed and slumped her shoulders, then realized something.

Sahara was utterly unresponsive in the scripture. She didn't give a single hint of Guiding Force reaction.

The scripture Menou currently carried under her left arm was Momo's. She felt the scripture containing Sahara at the bottom of her bag.

Sahara's lack of mockery felt fishy. Menou was suspicious, but she couldn't very well speak to the scripture in front of Ashuna.

"Now, I wonder, were you right about Momo being here? I'm looking forward to this."

"That's what we're here to find out. *Not* to have fun, so I'd appreciate it if you tempered your expectations, please…"

As they conversed, Menou and Ashuna headed into the hot spring town where they suspected Momo might be found.

✳✳✳

"Well?"

Having broken into a mansion on the outskirts of town, Momo glared down at the person at her feet.

"Would you mind telling me what exactly happened yesterday? I've already got plenty of evidence against you."

The man she had mercilessly tied up with her wirelike coping saw was the manager of the inn where she and Akari were staying. While Akari was convinced they had just been attacked by a series of unrelated sex offenders the day before, the insightful Momo sensed there was something more sinister behind it.

"You are the Recruiter, are you not? So why would you hire people to attack us, hmm? I may be a white-clad aide, but it should still be obvious that I belong to the Faust. Why couldn't you leave well enough alone?"

"L-like I'm ever gonna tell you...!"

Just as Momo suspected, they really hadn't been common criminals. The assault had occurred *because* she was part of the Faust. From the men's point of view, a girl in priestess's robes had shown up shortly before they were to welcome their recently escaped Director. Even if she was just an assistant priestess, it was only natural to assume that the Faust had caught wind of their plans and sent someone to intercept.

However, this was an unfortunate misunderstanding that only resulted in drawing Momo's attention to them.

"I see. Let me ask you another question, then."

Momo wasn't terribly insistent on learning why they had been attacked. Instead, she stated the main reason she'd tracked down the underworld businessman called the Recruiter.

"Hand over the list of your clients."

The bound man remained silent.

His role was to gather up criminals and give them work. He would never spill secrets about associates, even if tortured or threatened with death.

Momo regarded his determined expression with something like amusement. Her eyes glittered sadistically, like a cat licking its lips before toying with a dying mouse.

She drew out her favored weapon from the frilly hem of her skirt.

It was the second one she carried, the first being the one she'd used to bind the man. The grating, metallic sound it made hinted that it was designed not for cutting or for tying, but for sawing. She had chosen this weapon specifically to make her enemies suffer.

"Well, let's see how long you can hold out, then. I might not look it, but I got rather high marks in both torture and interrogation."

Most people could only tolerate so much pain, even if they're fully prepared to die.

Momo was aware of that as she began to move the saw.

"So I've found our next target."

A little while later, Momo returned from her morning escapade and relayed the events of the day to Akari.

The lost lamb stared at Momo in growing horror as she described exactly how she'd gotten information out of the Recruiter.

"Uh, Momo…"

The methods would have made even the hardened criminals

THE EXECUTIONER AND HER WAY OF LIFE, VOL. 4

of this town turn pale. Akari shook her head in disbelief at the heinous crimes against humanity the other girl casually described.

"Don't you have a single shred of a conscience or compassion or any of those nice C words? How do you even look at yourself in the mirror?"

"Whatever do you mean?" Momo tilted her head, looking genuinely at a loss for what the alleged issue was with her actions. "I just brought down a criminal group that attacked us first. Then I acquired the information necessary to root them out completely. If anything, you ought to be congratulating me on accomplishing both in such a short time."

"Oh really...?"

"Yes, really. I have no doubt that my darling would be patting me on the head and praising me right now."

"Oh *really*?"

The results alone seemed all right, but Akari couldn't help feeling like Momo had gone overboard. At the very least, she seriously doubted that Menou would have wholeheartedly approved of such methods.

Still, Akari wasn't overly interested in Momo's victims, either.

"So what are we going to do now?"

"I thought we could exterminate the rest of the Fourth scum and get you some training in the process," Momo said, offering a rather disturbing plan in the tone one might use to suggest a light stroll after a bath.

Akari wrinkled her nose.

"More of your so-called combat training? I don't want to do that..."

Akari wasn't the type to willfully engage in violence.

In the face of her evident reluctance, Momo devised another strategy.

"The Fourth is the group who drove my darling into a corner in Libelle. If we leave them alone, they'll try to hurt her again."

"We can't let that happen! Let's burn them to the ground!"

That was enough to get Akari completely on board. The Fourth members in this town were about to be in great peril.

"I was able to get information about the remaining Fourth members, some institutions that have committed various taboos, and so forth. Come with me, and we'll eradicate them one by one."

"You got it!"

Watching Akari nod vigorously, Momo knew her plan was going smoothly.

She was going to train Akari to lessen the burden on Menou. At least, that was what she'd said to convince Akari.

Her actual objective was to get Akari to overuse her Pure Concept.

Momo had no way to get rid of Akari, for the ordinary methods wouldn't kill her, and Menou's plan of using the Sword of Salt required passing through the holy land. Since Momo was currently on the run from her superior, she couldn't go with that option, either.

What was Momo to do, then?

She had reached a very different conclusion from Menou. All it would take was turning Akari into a Human Error.

By deceiving Akari into using her Pure Concept under the

guise of combat training, Momo intended to make her consume all her memories.

Menou's ultimate goal as an Executioner was to prevent anyone else from getting hurt. A Human Error was the worst situation imaginable for her.

Momo had been following Menou's directions, but her course had changed drastically upon hearing everything from Akari.

If Akari Tokitou became a Human Error, there were bound to be casualties. She could even wipe out an entire town.

And once Akari's Pure Concept went out of control, she would lose her sense of self.

There was no returning from that, extinguishing any hope of saving her. The holy land might even dispatch an entire squad to destroy the Human Error, instead of Menou having to do it alone. She would be relieved of the duty, and thus she would have no reason to betray the Faust to save Akari.

Of course, that would mean Menou had failed her mission, but it wouldn't cost her life. The punishment for Momo's solo escapade would likely be no worse than being reduced to a nun, either.

It was undoubtedly much better than letting Akari continue to turn back time repeated with no apparent hope of succeeding. *Regression* was far from risk-free, too. If she kept rewinding time, it might set Pandæmonium free completely.

It was a question of which would be worse: Akari becoming a Human Error or Pandæmonium's seal being released.

The only drawback was that there was no telling what kind of Human Error Akari might turn into, but Pandæmonium's threat was historically proven. She was one of the monstrous Four Major Human Errors that once destroyed an ancient civilization.

Her pinky alone had wrought plenty of destruction.

If the seal on the fog was broken completely, she might literally consume the world. That was certainly what happened to the Alliance of Southern Islands, land and all.

As long as Momo kept starting fights in this town and forcing Akari to use her Pure Concept conjurings, the girl's memories would eventually be used up. Once she didn't have enough left to use *Regression* on the entire world, the seal on the fog would loosen no more. Momo had come here because the village was isolated in the mountains. There were many tourists, but since it was a primarily Commons town, there were no important facilities nearby. If Akari became a Human Error here, it would only mean the annihilation of a single village.

Momo wasn't as kind as Menou. She simply chose the method most likely to save her darling's life.

As she gazed coolly at Akari's face in profile, Momo realized something.

"...This will be my first time killing an Otherworlder."

Momo was an Executioner's assistant.

She had slain no small amount of people.

But she had never actually executed an Otherworlder before. That was partially because there were so few of them to begin with, but it was also due to the fact that Menou didn't want to let Momo harm "good, innocent people."

So Momo had never killed anyone innocent of heresy.

Stepping onto the path of taboos meant deviating from morality, whether a lot or a little. A taboo was anything that required too many sacrifices, like Orwell's experiments on countless citizens.

Otherworlders were different, however.

It was all too clear to Momo, even in this short period of time, that Akari was different.

Whether Momo liked her or not, Akari was objectively a good person.

"Did you say something, Momo?"

"I did not. It must be your rotten ears hearing things."

"What do you mean, rotten?!"

Ignoring Akari, Momo sank into contemplation.

By now, Menou had likely finished saving money and would start her pursuit in earnest. They could only stay here for another three days or so. Once they ran out of criminals to fight, they would have to move on to the next place.

Pushing down the guilt that rose in her chest, Momo continued scheming to make Akari use up her memories.

Once they arrived at the inn, Sahara was left in a room with the luggage.

She was being literally treated like an object. Sahara fervently complained about Menou a hundred times in her mind, but there was no one to listen to her woes. After all, there was no need for Menou to walk around with the scripture that contained Sahara. She had the one Momo had left behind and naturally opted to use it instead of her own.

Thus, Sahara had been abandoned like unwanted refuse.

Menou had left to search for Momo and Akari, as planned.

Ashuna, who came to the hotel with Menou, was gone, too. That, at least, was a profound relief.

At that moment, Menou and Ashuna were serious threats to Sahara.

Left alone, Sahara's thoughts churned.

She had realized something at that rest area and wondered if it was worth informing Menou about her presence. However, Sahara abandoned that line of thought almost immediately.

Helping Menou in any way was meaningless. If she was in trouble, Sahara truly hoped it would be as difficult for her as possible. So long as Menou was keeping Sahara's existence from Ashuna a secret, that would work out perfectly.

What was there for her to do now, though?

Sahara's spirit drifted into deep consideration.

Existing within the scripture was a bizarre feeling. Despite the lack of a physical body, her consciousness remained, which should have been impossible. It was upon discovering that her mind was contained inside a scripture that she understood exactly what kind of Guiding vessel the scripture was.

Sahara was without her own form. In theory, that should have meant she no longer possessed the five senses and couldn't get any information about the outside world. She could produce her own appearance with the scripture conjuring that made a Guiding Light projection, but that was just an illusion. It had no physicality with which to hear or speak.

That was the reason that a body, soul, and spirit were all considered necessary parts of the definition of life.

Scriptures possessed a function that collected data, enabling Sahara to do the same. Curiously, however, it wasn't Sahara's will that was collecting said information.

The scripture was a Guiding vessel that existed to collect knowledge about the world.

By taking over that scripture's feature, Sahara learned about what was going on beyond her confines. In that sense, from the moment Sahara became part of the scripture, it lost its original function.

Everyone knew that a scripture was a complicated conjuring tool. At the same time, because it was so advanced, there was almost no one even in the church who understood all of its abilities.

Why did the scriptures exist? Why were they so specialized in gathering data that they could even preserve a soul and spirit?

Surely it wasn't to create beings like Sahara. Only priestesses approved by the Faust were allowed to carry one. They had to hone their Guiding Force aptitude and diligently study conjurings before they were given a scripture with which to work for churches throughout the land.

What was the purpose of providing the priestesses scattered across the continent with items that automatically collected information?

Now that Sahara was in this state, she began to question things that had never occurred to her before.

Regrettably, there wasn't a single thing she could do about it.

She seemed to be able to use some of the scripture's conjurings, but that didn't matter if she couldn't move. She existed only to be shoved to the bottom of a bag and carried around where no one would see her. And once she was brought to the holy land, she would be taken away from Menou.

Sahara didn't like this one bit.

The situation was far from optimal, and she couldn't even labor to better it.

No matter what she might figure out, it would all end in vain. That was immensely frustrating.

She even contemplated using a conjuring to destroy the room at the inn. It wouldn't really change anything, but it would at least be a good inconvenience.

As her thoughts strayed down a dangerous path, she heard the door to the room open.

Was Menou back? Sahara turned her attention toward the entrance and discovered that the guest was a young girl.

She appeared to be no more than ten years old and had probably entered the wrong room by mistake. Her footsteps were light and carefree as she strolled in.

The kid looked around slowly. Did she not realize yet that this wasn't her room? She tottered over to the corner where the luggage was gathered, drawing closer to Sahara.

Why was she able to unlock the door and enter the room if it wasn't hers? Sahara wondered if Ashuna had forgotten to lock the door, but the child was so young that she didn't register as a threat.

The little girl picked up the scripture without hesitation, probably intending to play some kind of game. She must have realized that this wasn't her room since the luggage wasn't hers. Sahara thought the kid was very poorly behaved.

Even if it was just a child's prank, though, being stolen away would be a problem for Sahara. If she used the image-conjuring feature of the scripture, she could at least pretend to be a ghost or something. Before she could enact the plan to scare off the intruder, the girl exclaimed something in pure glee.

"I found yooou. I knew I sensed the presence of *Vessel*

somewhere, and I was right! Maybe I'm still good for something after all, huh?"

Sahara's thoughts froze.

The child spoke of the Pure Concept of *Vessel*.

Sahara knew very well that *Vessel* referred to the Mechanical Society, one of the Four Major Human Errors. Anyone who knew that name couldn't just be an ordinary child.

The unfamiliar child gave an innocent giggle. Her cherubic face possessed elegant features with black hair and black eyes. There were three round holes on the front of her simple white dress.

"That lady was so silly to leave something so wonderful just lying around. Mm, but I guess maybe she doesn't quite know what you are, either. Even if scriptures are based on *Ivory*, the only concepts that can mess with the shape of a soul are *Vessel* and me, you know?"

The little girl was obviously aware of Sahara's existence and speaking to her directly. Sahara didn't respond, but the girl kept talking.

"I don't know who you are, but hello, nice to meet you. You must have prayed to you-know-who, am I right? If you hadn't, there's no way you would have wound up in this weird state. I know scriptures exist to complement the spirit, but I can only think of one person who could seal a soul in there. It's their fault you've ended up like this, too."

In essence, the Mechanical Society that eroded away at Sahara really just made any wishes that were offered to it come true. It entered the body, then the soul, and finally the spirit, assimilating with the target while granting their wish.

When the girl accurately assessed her situation, Sahara finally resigned herself. She manipulated her Guiding Force to activate a scripture conjuring, and the Guiding Light formed an image.

"...Who are you?"

"Mm! What a surprise."

Seeing the palm-sized Sahara, the girl exclaimed with all the delight of a child glimpsing a fairy in a dream. Her reaction seemed so deliberate that it irritated Sahara.

"Are you messing around or what?"

"Mm-mm, don't get mad, okay? I don't think it really matters who I am. If someone I don't know was already aware of me, I'd be disappointed."

"Disappointed...?"

"Mm-hmm! Because I'm really weak, you see. Compared to that *Vessel* person, I have to admit I'm a total weakling. But even so, I swear! I'll prove I can make someone's wish come true, too!"

Even as the girl clenched her fists and made a show of determination, her actions still seemed a little intentionally embellished. Based on her way of speaking, Sahara hazarded a guess at who the kid really was.

"Are you Pandæmonium?"

"Yep, that's right!"

The girl promptly nodded at Sahara's question. She was the worst and vilest of the Human Errors. The Master of all the evil and monsters in the world lifted the holy scripture with both hands.

"Now then, my dear little fairy friend." Pandæmonium

smiled earnestly at the bodiless Sahara and whispered, "Will you tell me what you want most of all?"

Sahara wanted to be somebody.

As her envy toward the rest of the world smoldered in her chest, the incarnation of Original Sin sparked the whole thing aflame.

As soon as she brought Ashuna to the inn, Menou promptly changed back into her priestess's robes.

Ashuna wanted to try the hot spring right away. Menou declined her invitation to come along and set out into town to gather information in her search for Momo.

The first place she went was the station, the main entry point for the village.

When Menou and Ashuna had arrived, the former was still dressed as a butler and waiting on the princess, so she'd decided it would seem too suspicious if she tried to ask anyone for information right away.

People were far more likely to trust someone in a priestess's attire.

That was especially true since the person she was searching for was clad in a white robe, the garb of an assistant priestess. Menou was wearing the indigo robes of an official priestess, making it easy for her to say she was looking for her subordinate without garnering any suspicion.

"Oh yes, I saw someone like that. She's traveling with another girl, right? They got off at this station three days ago. I remember it well because they seemed so incredibly upset with each other."

While asking around with employees, Menou hit upon an eyewitness on her second try.

Akari and Momo were bound to stand out unless they made a serious effort to hide. Momo could have at least changed her clothes, but she must have wanted to take advantage of people's trust in priestesses, too. With that valuable information, Menou thanked the employee and started walking.

It was all but certain that Momo was somewhere in this town. She had to be operating under the assumption that her attempt to slow Menou down monetarily was a success. Judging by her lack of effort to cover her tracks or disguise herself, it was obvious that Momo's guard was down.

"She's much too careless…"

Perhaps Momo was due for reeducation on that front.

Still, this worked to Menou's advantage. If she guessed their inn based on Momo's budget, she might actually locate them quite quickly.

Menou stood in an empty area near the station, gathering her thoughts about where to go next when someone suddenly called out to her from behind.

"Pardon me, lovely lady, might I have a moment of your time?"

The voice was polite yet had a hint of teasing in the tone. Menou was confident she had heard it somewhere before, but she couldn't immediately connect it to a face, a rarity for her.

Searching her memories as she turned around, Menou's eyes fell on a kimono-clad young woman with luxurious deep-blue hair hanging in a thick braid over her shoulder.

"You're…"

At Menou's reaction, the girl unfolded her trademark iron fan and held it to her lips with a mischievous smile.

"...Manon."

"Hello again, Ms. Menou."

Manon Libelle was a girl who Menou had met in the port city of Libelle and later impaled with a blade.

The surprise only lasted for a moment. Then Menou shifted to wariness.

"Truly, I am so pleased to see you again. Yes, it is I, Manon, the negative form of evil."

"...And what is that supposed to mean? That you're the person who accompanies Pandæmonium?"

"Hee-hee. I'm quite fond of that introduction, actually."

Menou was taken aback by Manon's mysterious epithet and her friendly demeanor. The priestess readied herself to draw her dagger at a moment's notice as she cautiously responded.

"It's been a while. I heard you might have helped the Director escape from Grisarika, but it's still disappointing to see that you really are still alive."

"More or less. Technically, I died and was brought back to life, but I suppose it doesn't really matter. I, Manon Libelle, have been revived from the depths of the underworld."

Menou had also heard from Momo that Pandæmonium resurrected Manon as a demon.

The situation wasn't all that different from Sahara's. Manon's physical body was dead, but her soul and spirit survived in another vessel.

Pandæmonium controlled the Pure Concept of *Evil*. It was the basis of all Original Sin Conjurings and could mold and break the body, spirit, and soul that made up life like so much clay.

"…It was Pandæmonium who brought you back, wasn't it?"

"Yes, that's correct."

Menou thought back to her encounter with Manon in Libelle. When Pandæmonium had appeared, Manon split apart from the inside and was torn open, clearly spelling the end of her life. On top of that, her body had been consumed by a monster afterward.

In retrospect, Pandæmonium must have done that to preserve Manon's soul.

"Where is she now?"

"Who knows?"

Manon didn't appear to be playing dumb. She slowly tapped a finger on her chin as if contemplating Pandæmonium's whereabouts.

"I'm sure she's out amusing herself. She is a willful little thing, and I do not wish to inhibit her, so I let her do as she pleases."

"…I see. So what is it you want?"

Allowing Pandæmonium to run free was a terrifying concept.

Manon was now the very definition of a taboo. Surely she hadn't shown herself in front of an Executioner like Menou just to make small talk.

"I'd especially like to know why you chose to make direct contact with me. I imagine it would be much more convenient for you if I thought you were dead… You must have an excellent reason for forfeiting that advantage, yes?"

"Nothing so specific. I didn't like being left alone in a room with a freak, so I went outside and just happened to run into you by chance, that's all."

"By chance…?" Menou repeated.

"Yes. And I called out to you because I thought it would bother you more if I came to see you so directly."

While watching Menou's brow furrow, Manon put a sleeve to her mouth and chuckled lightly.

"I do so love how frank you are, Ms. Menou. You're much too good a person to be an Executioner. That much is for certain."

Manon claimed she had shown herself instead of sneaking around to keep her existence a secret purely to get under Menou's skin. That assertive attitude, so at odds with her gentle appearance, was typical Manon. After all, she had offered her family and followers as sacrifices to Pandæmonium simply because she was in her "rebellious phase"—or so she'd claimed at the time.

"Besides, it seems that the Faust is already aware of my existence, so there would be no point in attempting to conceal it."

"…Are you up to something in this town? This approach is quite different from your actions in Libelle."

"Oh, no, we really did only stop here to rest. It appears there are a surprising number of unusual visitors right now, but that is truly just happenstance."

While Menou still didn't let down her guard, Manon continued to speak lightly.

"But since we've run into each other, could I ask you a little favor? You are aware that Ms. Momo is also here, right?"

"…Yes, I certainly am."

Menou had come here to pursue Momo.

If Manon knew about that predicament, that meant she knew Akari was here, too. Depending on Manon's goals, Momo's separation from Menou might prove to be a fatal mistake.

It was even possible that the two had already fallen into Manon's hands. Menou was so deeply suspicious that Manon's next words caught her entirely by surprise.

"Ms. Momo has been bullying the Fourth members in this town. I don't suppose you could stop her for me?"

"Excuse me?" Menou accidentally stammered. "Momo... bullying...? What do you mean?"

"You'll have to find out the details for yourself."

Since her imagination had been running in a dark direction, Menou was more confused than anything. Manon was really throwing everything on Menou, despite her calling it a little favor.

"I am not terribly interested in Ms. Momo myself, so I do not want to cause conflict. I doubt she would listen to anything I ask of her, but it is getting to the point where I cannot just stand by and let her carry on... But I doubt fighting her would be very exciting for me. Thus, I thought it might be best to leave it in your hands instead."

"Wouldn't most people prefer not to fight people they *are* interested in?"

"Do you think so? But don't you want the person you like to spend time on you in some way?"

This was incredibly difficult logic to follow. Mentally groaning, Menou nevertheless continued the conversation in the hopes of gaining more information.

"Back to the matter at hand, the Faust hold poor influence in this region. As such, there are a fair amount of Fourth supporters here. They even use the area for the occasional meeting."

"Are you giving me this information so I can weed them all out?"

"Well, it doesn't really matter now, as they were already half wiped out by the time I arrived." Manon shook her head. Judging by the context, Momo must have been responsible. "I thought the easiest way to tidy things up would be to have you get her under control, Ms. Menou. So I came to tell you about Ms. Momo in hopes that you might retrieve her right away."

"...You aren't going to save your Fourth comrades?"

"Oh, we are not allies by any means. I only wish for my own freedom. I have no interest in revolutionizing the caste system or anything like that. The Faust, the Noblesse, the Commons... With or without such divisions, there shall always be people like me."

People like Manon.

The girl who had fallen into taboo and sacrificed all her blood relatives giggled lightly.

"If there is anything I do wish to devote myself to... Well, let me think. Were someone to seek a way to fundamentally solve the problem of lost ones, I would be happy to help them."

She cast Menou a meaningful glance, as if she was hoping that Menou might do just such a thing.

Ignoring her nonsense, Menou shifted back to the main subject.

"One way or another, I will be collecting Momo, yes. But what I'm going to do about you is another story entirely."

"In that case, I do have a suggestion." While Menou shot her a hostile look, Manon only smiled back and clasped her hands together in apparent sincerity. "Won't you join me, Ms. Menou? I would be delighted to have you."

She made the invitation in the same natural tone as some-one starting a casual chat.

For a moment, Menou was dumbstruck, trying to process what she'd just been asked.

"...Are you serious?"

"Very much so. Ms. Akari and Ms. Momo are welcome to join us, too. It would be my pleasure."

Manon was serious. This made Menou wonder instead if the other girl was sane, but Manon looked wholly calm and intent.

It wasn't a bluff. Manon was genuinely suggesting to Menou that they join forces.

After overcoming her doubt, Menou moved on to amazement.

"You're asking me to join the Fourth?"

"Oh, no. The Fourth is an organization created by the Director, and it's quite rotten by now. They are worth taking advantage of, but I see no significance to their activities. Evidently, the local members are mostly sex offenders anyway," she replied, voice dropping to a whisper at the last part. "So no, don't worry about the Fourth. I would like you to join me as a personal ally with a shared ideal; that is all."

An individual associate.

If Manon wanted partners, that meant she must have a specific goal, not just committing crimes on impulse.

Menou had to find out more. With Pandæmonium on her side, Manon was not to be underestimated.

"Why would you invite me? I killed you in Libelle, as I recall."

"I do not resent you for that in the least, Ms. Menou. You did thoroughly defeat me, but I still managed to accomplish my goal."

This made sense.

Menou emerged victorious in the fight, but Manon had already succeeded in making herself a taboo.

Everything after the events in Libelle was nothing more than a diversion. Manon even went into her fight with Menou fully prepared to die.

Still, it was strange that she wouldn't have a single ounce of resentment about being killed.

"Either way, I'll have to decline. I am a priestess, remember."

"Are you sure? I'm quite certain other wonderful allies are waiting for you, too."

"Don't be absurd. I'm an Executioner. I haven't fallen so far as to get involved with taboos, and if I betrayed my position, I myself would be hunted down by the Faust. How could I possibly accept?"

If Manon genuinely was hoping to recruit Menou, she was giving a poor show of it. There was nothing to sway the priestess's position.

Manon looked unruffled; perhaps she had been anticipating this response. She muttered "I see..." in faint disappointment, then carried on the conversation with her expression unchanged.

"She told you there's a way, I hear."

"Come again?"

"A way to kill Ms. Akari. I'm told she whispered to you that it's the Sword of Salt."

What was this girl getting at? Menou couldn't help falling quiet, unsure where the sudden change in topic was leading.

Manon cut into the silence after a moment.

"Allow me to offer you a piece of advice as well."

"Nothing you say could possibly—"

"There's another way to prevent Otherworlders from going berserk."

Menou's mind went blank.

Her voice died out midsentence. She couldn't even keep her expression from reacting.

"...You're lying."

When she finally choked out a short sentence, her voice was so fragile it didn't sound like her own.

Manon gave an elegant titter. "I'm not. Think about it, Ms. Menou. A thousand years ago, Pure Concepts helped develop a civilization. Instead of eliminating them as we do now, our world accepted Otherworlders and walked with them side by side. It's clear that ancient peoples didn't climb to triumph by abusing the Otherworlders, either. Why else would our language have become so close to theirs?"

What did this mean?

"That could only happen if we interacted with them incredibly closely for a long time... Or it could even be that the Otherworlders were considered superior, or their words would never have taken over ours. So why were we able to do such a thing?"

Manon gazed directly into Menou's eyes.

"It's true, isn't it? When Otherworlders use their Pure Concepts, they lose their memories. Eventually, they even forget their own names, and become monstrous slaves to their concepts. Such unstable beings could never become part of the ruling class. So why were the Otherworlders of those times so

THE EXECUTIONER AND HER WAY OF LIFE, VOL. 4

accepted that the language of this world became unified with Japanese?"

Menou could offer no objection. The theory made sense. There were no apparent holes in Manon's assertions.

"Thus, there must have been a way. A system that prevented Otherworlders from losing control must have existed."

"This is all just hypothetical. Even if it was true in that era, it's meaningless if it's gone now."

"How can you be so sure that it is?"

"It's obvious."

Manon's claim certainly didn't inspire any hope in Menou, because even if her claim was true, Menou would still have to kill Akari.

If there was a way to let Otherworlders exist without killing them, the upper ranks of the Faust would have to know about it. Menou was a member of the Faust, an Executioner who hunted taboos. She had no right to rebel against the ironclad rules.

Even if there was a way to save her, Menou still had to kill Akari unless her orders changed.

It was her duty.

Akari wasn't Menou's first target. She had already murdered a considerable number of Otherworlders.

If a system like that was real, and the top brass of the Faust were hiding it...

Then what was the meaning of all the corpses that Menou had added to the heap over her life?

"Furthermore, I believe there is a way to travel from this world to that one."

"That's even more ridiculous. Even the ancient civilization has no records of an Otherworlder returning home."

Manon brushed off Menou's instinctive reaction.

"It's not like you to let your emotions rule your responses, Ms. Menou. Do you know how conjurings came to be? Dig around the roots, and you'll find out soon enough. And there is a meaning behind it. The system of our society permits the removal of outside enemies if it is deemed beneficial. For instance, let me see…" She gave an almost exaggerated smile. "If the Elders—the highest members of the Faust and its decision-making body—defined any intruders from another world as enemies, it would be considered just to destroy them."

Menou forced her agitated feelings back to calm herself, then licked her dry lips. "Say whatever you like, but it's all talk. I'd have to see evidence before I believe your theory."

"That's unsurprising. I'm about to start collecting the evidence, so I don't have it just yet, but…think about it, Ms. Menou." Manon smiled enchantingly. "Would there be any reason to protect them? Why would the powerful people who established our society's system safeguard lost lambs with no connection to anyone and overwhelming power? Even if you kill an Otherworlder, they have no family in this world."

Otherworlders were those with no place to go.

They possessed no family, no friends, no neighbors. Not a single familiar face in all the world. Since they wandered into this place alone, no one noticed when they disappeared.

That was why the violent method of having Executioners dispose of them was given a pass. Since even summoning them was a sin, the people who had done so would hold their tongues. And so the Faust continued slaying all the lost ones who came to this world with little resistance.

"Shall I give you a hint?"

"No, thank you."

"Otherworlders expend their memories, their personalities—in other words, their souls. What if something existed that could preserve those things?"

"But there's no such—," Menou started to reply, but then a sudden realization cut her short.

There *was* an object capable of that feat.

Menou just so happened to possess an item that perfectly fit Manon's description.

Something that retained memories and personality even with the physical body gone.

In other words, Sahara's current state.

What if that was why the scriptures existed in the first place?

"Ms. Menou. Do you remember what I said to you in Libelle?"

"What...do you mean?"

"Children can't help trying to live up to the expectations of the adults around them."

Before Menou could regain control over her thoughts, her mind thrown into chaos by the theory that arose, Manon continued in a quiet, mature tone.

"I took the liberty of investigating your past a little... You met Flare after you lost your memories, yes? She's the most successful taboo hunter in history, an Executioner and living legend. Perhaps you wanted to measure up to her example? It's common for young children to want to imitate the lifestyle of the person closest to them."

"She never...!" Menou's tone came out sharper than she intended. Realizing this, she quickly lowered her voice.

"She never asked anything of me."

"Regardless, that doesn't mean she didn't have an influence on you in some way." Manon's voice suggested she had gone through the exact same thing once. "A guardian has a profound effect on a child just by being around them."

However, Menou's childhood was nothing like Manon's. The latter was the child of an Otherworlder and thus saddled with high expectations and treated as a disappointment when she failed to meet them.

And yet Manon seemed to empathize with the other young woman.

"Ms. Menou, I think it would be best if you learned your true identity."

"My identity?"

"Yes. Your roots. That will help you find your path in life. The reason I am traveling with Pandæmonium is deeply connected to my own birth, too."

Manon had the blood of an Otherworlder. The events she caused in Libelle and her motivation for releasing Pandæmonium were both tied to that fact.

"Allow me to ask you one more time, Ms. Menou..." Manon peered into Menou's face. "If you knew there was a way to save her, would you still kill Ms. Akari?"

Menou struggled to answer right away. Her face was no longer that of a coolheaded Executioner, but of her true self.

The part of her that was faint and fragile, so unlike the sharp blade she had honed herself to be.

Manon's eyes softened. Full of fondness for Menou's inner weakness, she invited her again.

"Ms. Menou. Join forces with me, and we'll find a way to save Ms. Akari together. You said it yourself, didn't you? You claimed you're a villain. That means you know it's wrong to kill Ms. Akari."

Manon held out her hand.

"Please, Ms. Menou."

A silence settled over the pair for a few moments.

"...Manon."

"Yes?"

Just as Manon responded to the quiet call, there was a flash.

"Do I...really seem that weak to you?"

It was a blade.

Menou closed the distance between them in an instant, drawing her dagger from her thigh and tackling the other girl.

As she drew breath, Menou invoked Guiding Enhancement. Her weapon closed toward Manon's throat in the blink of an eye.

Still on the ground, Manon deflected the attack with a snap of her fan. At the same time, her shadow formed into a blade, which Menou evaded by jumping aside.

"Now that's the Ms. Menou I know! You never hesitate, do you?"

"Why should I? If you are still alive after committing a taboo—I'll just have to kill you again."

Manon appeared strangely pleased about Menou's attack. She stood up while Menou steadied herself and readied her iron fan.

Menou narrowed her eyes at the other girl's posture.

"You've certainly changed, though. You're much stronger now."

"Oh, yes. The base parts for my new body were quite exceptional, so I've naturally become more skilled."

Manon's Guiding Force flowed through her feet and into the ground.

"Do you remember this?"

Guiding Force: Connect—Shadow, Pseudo-Concept [Null]—Invoke [Nullshadow]

Manon's shadow pierced through Menou's barrier.

"These were people you killed in Grisarika."

Pseudo-Concepts.

These were conjurings received if one used material from a Pure Concept holder. The *Null* concept could only have come from the boy Menou killed in Grisarika Kingdom.

Menou immediately recognized the nature of the conjuring Manon had acquired, but still she didn't falter.

"You really think you can defeat me with just that?"

A shadow containing the Pseudo-Concept of *Null*. Body movements that had become highly polished. Manon was certainly a more formidable opponent now.

Even that wouldn't be enough to beat Menou in a one-on-one fight, however.

"Manon. You said you want me to become a personal ally. What do you seek that's so different from the Fourth?"

"Ah yes, I suppose I hadn't mentioned that yet."

Their exchange continued even as they sought to kill each other. Manon was surprisingly quick to reply.

"I want to change the way that lost ones live. I am now the only person in the world who knows what that girl was like before she became Pandæmonium, after all."

Her tone was heavy and profound.

What did that mean? Menou looked at Manon questioningly, but the girl merely covered her mouth with her fan.

"Hee-hee. Well, you know. At the moment, my primary goal is to try going to the other world."

A method of going to another world, instead of summoning someone from there.

Menou, too, had once questioned whether such a thing existed.

"And you think that's a way to solve the issue of lost ones?"

"I believe it might be one possible answer."

"There is no method of traveling from this world to the other."

Menou bluntly rejected this theory. She had asked, long ago, whether it could be done. And her Master had firmly told the young Menou that it could not.

Yet Manon smiled brightly as she continued to argue.

"Oh, but I have very reliable information. It's based on what I've been told by Pandæmonium, the Director...and your Master, Flare."

"...You met her?"

"I did, indeed. Not that long ago. Did you not hear about the town we destroyed recently?"

The idea that Manon had destroyed a settlement was not particularly shocking. She was traveling with Pandæmonium, even if it was just her pinky finger. Any defenseless village beset upon by the incarnation of Original Sin had little chance of surviving.

The problem was that she had met Master Flare there.

When faced with a taboo, Menou's Master would invariably execute the perpetrator. However, if Manon was still alive, that meant she had become strong enough to successfully escape from Master Flare.

"She told me all kinds of interesting things. It was well worth the effort of crushing that town, if you ask me."

"……"

Menou's Guiding Enhancement suddenly cut off. Dropping such a necessary source of strength in the middle of battle was an unmistakably bad move. Sensing that the threat had lessened, Manon hesitated to react for just a moment in her confusion, and Menou used that opportunity to lunge at her.

Even without Guiding Enhancement, her trained movements were remarkably sharp. Manon's shadow rose instinctively. Since it contained a portion of her spirit and soul as an extension of her body, her shadow had become a weapon that moved however the girl willed it.

The shade formed a swathe of ebon blades and attempted to block the dagger, but Menou had anticipated as much.

Scripture, 3:1—Invoke [And the oncoming enemy did hear the tolling of the bell.]

The ringing bell of "power" scattered Manon's shadow.

Without anything left to bar her way, Menou swung down her dagger. Manon braced herself to block it with her fan. The priestess didn't have Guiding Enhancement on her side, since she was prioritizing a surprise maneuver, leaving Manon confident that she could catch the attack.

She was wrong.

Guiding Force: Connect—Dagger Crest—Invoke [Gale]

Before the two armaments collided, a gust of wind erupted from Menou's dagger and raced toward Manon, knocking her to the ground. Menou immediately took position above her and thrust the scripture toward her.

She was going to be killed.

147

But even in the moment of her certain victory, Menou never let her guard down.

All the while, she remained aware that Pandæmonium was nowhere to be seen. Even as she formed a scripture conjuring to finish off Manon, she watched her surroundings, ready for an interruption to appear at any time, from anywhere.

She was prepared to react the moment she detected a presence behind her.

Instead of being caught by surprise, Menou only felt vindicated. The Executioner jumped away from Manon at once and immediately turned to thrust her blade into—

"...Huh?"

Her weapon stopped short of Sahara, who was standing in front of Menou wearing a nun's habit, something that should have been impossible. It was the real thing; Sahara had a proper body.

Menou couldn't believe her eyes. Her blade trembled with shock at the unpredicted arrival.

How could Sahara be here, moving with a physical body?

"Well, that's a fine way to say hello, Menou."

While Menou couldn't fully process her surprise, Sahara knocked her blade aside with her right arm, her eyes looking sleepy as usual. The impact knocked Menou off-balance, while Sahara clenched her metal hand with a clang.

"This is what you get for shoving me in the bottom of your bag."

Sahara's fist struck Menou squarely in the stomach.

Her right arm was a silvery Guiding prosthetic, just as it had been before she'd been sealed in the scripture. The attack from her metal arm was so unnatural that it seemed to move her body rather than the other way around, but it was still on par with a punch from Momo with Guiding Enhancement.

"Nngh…!"

Menou's face contorted in pain. Maybe she shouldn't have raised her leg to lessen the force of the blow. The unexpected power of the strike had sent Menou's body flying into the air, unable to regain control immediately.

Why was Sahara here—and with a body of her own? Menou looked around in midair to try to gather information and spotted the cause immediately.

Pandæmonium was standing behind Sahara. Evidently noticing Menou's gaze, she smiled brightly and waved.

Oh, great.

Menou grimaced as she theorized how Sahara had obtained a new body. It was the same method that had granted Manon one. No, perhaps the particulars of the technique were different. Either way, it was undoubtedly a similar approach.

Pandæmonium used an Original Sin Conjuring to give Sahara a physical form.

"You can have this back."

Just before Menou landed, Sahara tossed over a scripture, the one her soul and spirit had been inside.

"I know I asked you to kill me before, but this time around…"

Guiding Force: Merge Materials—Prosthetic Arm, Inner Seal Conjuration—

Sahara's artificial arm sparkled with Guiding Light. It concentrated around her fist, obeying the conjuring she was creating.

"I think I'd just like to see you try."

Activate [Skill: Guiding Cannon]

149

©nilitsu

Guiding Force: Connect—Priestess Robes, Crest—Invoke [Barrier]

Just before the blast of light struck, Menou used the crest hidden in her priestess robes to produce a protective barrier. It appeared diagonally and bounced the Guiding Cannon off into the sky.

Menou had luckily avoided fatal injuries, but she'd landed to find all three enemies, including Pandæmonium, out of her range.

"It's a pleasure to meet you. I'm Manon Libelle. What a lovely arm you have!"

"I'm Sahara. A former nun. My least favorite things are Menou and Momo. I'm in a great mood right now, since I just got to sock Menou one."

The two of them were nonchalantly introducing themselves. This was their first meeting, but their similarly laid-back personalities were meshing well. From the look of things, they hadn't been conspiring in secret prior.

"…Well, you two seem to be hitting it off," Menou muttered darkly. It was unclear how Sahara had made contact with Pandæmonium in such a short time.

The long sleeves of Manon's kimono fluttered as she waved a hand.

"What do you think? We could become a nice trio of friends now."

The idea wasn't even worth a moment's thought. Menou ignored Manon's proposal and addressed Sahara instead.

"Sahara. No good will come of following Manon."

"You say that like I'd be better off going with you." Sahara put a mechanical hand on her hip. "Even if I was on my best behavior, the most I could hope for is getting burned. Otherwise, I'd be subjected to experiments. Since I'm already considered a taboo, I might as well join this side, don't you think?"

Menou couldn't argue with that. Sahara didn't stand to gain anything by following Menou. She'd put off dealing with the situation because Sahara had been trapped, and nobody else knew about her—but Pandæmonium must have found out somehow.

Now there were two.

Menou glared at the pair of girls who had escaped death by her hand.

Defeating them was still possible.

She calmly assessed their abilities.

Menou knew Sahara's strength quite well, and she'd just fought against Manon, too. Even if they teamed up, Menou would have the upper hand. Pandæmonium was the only wild card, but she was still only a tiny portion of her full power—a pinky finger's worth, to be precise.

The Pure Concept of *Evil* was unique in that it required sacrifices to produce significant results. Manon had stated that she'd destroyed a town when she'd met Master Flare. She'd also mentioned that they came to this town to "rest."

If they'd used up all their sacrifices in their fight against Flare, perhaps they intended to restore that energy here. If so, then this was a once-in-a-lifetime opportunity to capture Pandæmonium's pinky finger.

Menou took a deep breath to heighten her concentration.

She could win this. She cast aside her doubts, gathered her confidence, and took a breath—when something hard suddenly jabbed into her back.

"Now, now, what do you think you're doing to my daughter?"

A shiver ran down her spine.

There was someone behind her. Even if she'd been focusing on the three in front of her, it was still unusual that she hadn't noticed this person at all until they were close enough to touch her. That alone was enough to make her shudder.

The object pressing into Menou's back felt cylindrical. It was most likely a Guiding gun. It would be difficult to escape unscathed if she was shot at point-blank distance like this.

Menou focused all her nerves on her back even as she took on a casual tone and spoke to Manon as calmly as she could.

"Manon... Since when is your father still alive?"

"Oh no. Please don't listen to a word that freak says."

Manon usually wore a gentle smile, regardless of the situation, but her expression was serious for once. With a gun to her back, Menou couldn't afford to ignore the man's words.

He spoke again.

"You must be Flarette, hmm? It is quite an honor to meet her successor."

"...And you are?"

"Ha-ha-ha. I'm under no obligation to tell you—"

"He's the Director."

Manon's smile returned as she revealed his identity. The haughty-sounding man fell silent at this betrayal.

"Miss Manon... I must say, er, I do have my own position to consider, you know. I do wish you would allow me to have my moment in the spotlight..."

"I don't care." Manon coolly brushed off his plea. "Whatever you think your status is, you're certainly not my father."

As this absurd conversation went on, Menou grew resigned to her death. There were three formidable opponents in front of her—and what was most likely a deadly weapon pressed against her back.

While Menou was bracing herself for a fight that would likely lead to defeat, the Director cleared his throat pointedly.

"Now then, Flarette. I have no intention of fighting you, nor do I intend to take your life. Truth be told, I would have much preferred to sit down and have a nice, long chat with Flare's successor... It's a shame we had to meet in this manner. I would appreciate it if you would peacefully withdraw."

"And if I refuse?"

"Ha-ha," the man said with a chuckle. It was a quiet, coiling laugh, like a snake slithering out of the darkness. "Surely you will not. You know what sort of person I am, don't you?"

His laughter echoed behind her.

Menou was indeed aware of the Director. This was a life-threatening situation.

The object pressed into her spine was presumably a Guiding gun. The Director's skillful approach had been undetectable. And most alarming of all was the fact that he'd fought against Menou's Master for many years.

"Since you are no doubt familiar with my history, I can't imagine you would ignore my request. You see, sometimes knowledge can feel like shackles. Often, the more enlightened someone is, the less they can move freely. Ignorance is a sin, but sometimes the wise can have more limited options than the foolish. You understand, do you not?"

Perhaps it was merely a threat. Maybe he didn't have enough time to prepare anything else.

Still, Menou certainly comprehended. She was all too aware of this man's deeds. She had heard how crafty he was in his ongoing clash with Master Flare. And so, even if she was on her guard, she couldn't risk ignoring him.

"Now, would you mind letting us go freely?"

Menou held back a snarl and nodded. Dying here would be a waste. Judging by the disappointed look on Sahara's face, it might have even worked out in her favor that her enemies had chosen to retreat.

"Well, thank you kindly! Ah, and worry not. The object at your back is nothing but an ordinary cane, hmm? I don't carry anything so dangerous as a Guiding gun."

This did make Menou snarl, but she wasn't even sure if she believed the Director's claim. He was still standing behind her. As Menou stood stock-still, Manon gave her a casual farewell.

"Alas, we'll have to cut our reunion short for now. I do hope you'll play with me again sometime, Ms. Menou."

"Sucks to be you, Menou... Oh, and let me give you a piece of advice." Her freedom restored, Sahara gleefully mocked Menou as if to make up for all her prior gloom. "I'm willing to bet that not a single thing is going to go the way you want in this town."

All Menou could do was watch as the trio of dangerous girls each teased her in their own unique manner and walked away.

CHAPTER 4
The Escape Reaches Its End

Mountains surrounded the hot springs town where Momo and Akari were staying.

Just one peak over from this relaxing tourist spot, there was a suspicious building in an undeveloped and rocky area. It was carefully stationed out of sight, for it was the site of taboo conjuring research. The analysts gathered there were attempting to develop new kinds of conjurings.

The Faust forbade any excessive probing into conjuring. Thus, researchers who devoted themselves to study or intense curiosity were already approaching a taboo. People whose field of investigation exceeded the boundaries set by the Faust gathered here to carry out their experiments.

At least, until two young girls destroyed the place.

"Honestly. How stupid can you get? I've never once heard of any efforts to develop new conjurings succeeding unless the Faust did it. What kind of senselessness possessed you to hide away out here and try it anyway?"

Momo's voice sounded cheerful. Over the past few days,

she'd been using the information she dragged out of the Recruiter to clear out every last villain in the area. She had already crushed the meeting places used by the Fourth, and as soon as she'd learned they were supporting a secret lab in the mountains, she'd broken in to give the researchers their own taste of hell.

A disturbing smile spread across Momo's adorable face as she glanced over the data from their studies.

"The fact that you would want to try something like this tells me what total failures you were. Really, nice job wasting your time on such pointless work, you losers."

"Oh? These people were doing meaningless research?"

"They certainly were. This isn't the kind of thing that unauthorized people could do anything about. Devoting your whole life to something that will never succeed is completely crazy."

On top of the physical beating, Momo went on mercilessly breaking their hearts as well, still wearing a sweet grin. Her harsh words were enough to drive the members of the research facility even further to the brink.

"Now, all that's left is to report this to the knights, and I suppose we'll be done. This area's certainly gotten a lot more peaceful now, hmm? It makes me proud to be a member of the Faust."

Looking like she was pleased with herself for doing a good deed, she tossed the last beaten-up analyst aside like an old rag. Momo's footsteps were light as air while they left the lab behind. Akari, who walked beside her, looked far more conflicted.

She had realized with growing alarm that while Momo was usually in a terrible mood whenever she was with her, the assistant Executioner always seemed to be much more cheerful after going on a violent rampage.

Despite her claim that this was all for Akari's "combat training," Momo had definitely knocked out far more victims. Akari began to suspect that she was just being dragged along in Momo's efforts to lift her own spirits.

"I know beating people up is your hobby and all, but... shouldn't you be a little more considerate?"

"This is my job, you know. Besides, I'm doing all this to train *you*. What could be more considerate?"

"Yeah, right. You're obviously enjoying this way more than me."

Akari narrowed her eyes as Momo insisted she was in the right.

The latter's pink hair bobbed along in pigtails. It was a non-naturally occurring color in the world Akari hailed from, but the people in this world had many different hair colors. Supposedly, it was influenced by genetics and the Guiding Force produced by each individual's soul. There were even a few schools of thought that a person's hair color could provide insights into their personality.

It wasn't necessarily any more accurate than the blood type–based assessments that were popular in Japan, but as Akari looked at Momo, she thought there might be something to it after all.

Warm colors like red were said to indicate a selfish and emotional person.

This was a piece of trivia Akari had heard from Menou in one of the previous time loops. She didn't know about anyone else, but it certainly suited Momo to a tee.

"So is it really that hard to research conjurings?"

"It's difficult enough to develop new additions to already-existing ones, and creating completely new conjuring forms is all but impossible. At the very least, I haven't heard of any successful attempts in the past few decades. The only recent advancement that comes to mind is the image-recording conjuring that was added to the scriptures about twenty years ago."

"Oh yeah? So new ones do come out every once in a while, then."

Since Akari didn't have detailed knowledge of the subject, she wasn't particularly interested. Thus, she only posed the question as a casual conversation topic.

"How are new conjurings like that made?"

"How? Well, obviously..."

Momo started to respond to the foolish question, then trailed off.

Unlike Akari, who could invoke conjurings on pure intuition, Momo had to study the fundamentals—namely, crestology and materialogy—in order to use crest and scripture conjurings.

However, since all her information was practical, she hadn't ever studied those subjects' history.

Akari was quick to notice Momo's lack of understanding.

"Ooh, so you don't know, either, Momo? Wow, you talk a big game for someone who clearly hasn't done their homework."

"...Quiet, you."

"Ha-ha-ha, it's so easy to tell when you're mad! Your face gets all— Oww?!"

As Akari moved to prod Momo's puffed-up cheeks, she found herself getting swatted away instead. Akari rubbed her hand where it had been smacked as she glowered at Momo out of the corner of her eye.

Akari's opinion of Momo had changed somewhat during their time together in this village.

She'd initially believed that Momo was just an annoying interloper. She always clung to Menou and viewed Akari as an enemy. That was the extent of Akari's impression of Momo, since they never had much direct contact in the first place. Momo stayed hidden from Akari during every time loop and followed her and Menou from a distance.

This was the first time they had interacted in such a long time.

"Hey, Momo."

"What is it?"

Momo responded with surprising politeness.

She wasn't actually as insanely violent as she let on. Momo's hostility toward Akari was genuine, but she would still answer if Akari tried to talk to her. It was a little annoying that she had never once referred to Akari by name, but her attitude was still comparatively harmless.

Momo only cared about saving Menou's life, and she didn't concern herself with anything else. Naturally, that included Akari.

Many of Akari's failures in previous time loops had involved assuming that Momo wasn't necessary.

With that knowledge in mind, Akari swallowed her pride and presented a piece of information the other girl might not know.

"Listen… What would you do if I told you there might be a way for me to go back to my old world?"

"Come again?" Momo looked dubious. "Where did you hear such a made-up rumor? There's no conjuring that can send people to the other world, as far as I know. And as I just said, new conjurings are difficult to create, remember?"

"Um, well, it was back in Libelle. I had a short conversation with Pandæmonium, just for a minute. And she told me there was a way to return."

"...Pandæmonium said that, did she?"

It was a full-on fight that Akari lost, not just a conversation, but she excluded that information for fear of being teased further.

Momo's expression wavered at this news.

"If that's the case, then...it might really be true."

Pandæmonium had been cut off from all else by an unbreakable seal for nearly a thousand years. If she said there was a conjuring to send Otherworlders back, then it couldn't be a recent development.

That would mean the method had to have existed for at least a millennium.

"Hmm. I know I'm the one who brought it up, but couldn't Pandæmonium just be lying?" questioned Akari.

"Human Errors cannot lie," Momo responded. "It's not just them, either—anyone whose spirit has been worn away can no longer conceive of deception."

Human Errors were a Pure Concept in human form. At first glance, they might seem to have a personality, but that was only on the surface.

The only impulses that moved a Human Error came from the concept that had taken over their soul and completely wore away their spirit to hijack their body.

"You never thought to tell my darling that there might be a way for you to go back?"

"I'd never heard of such a thing until Pandæmonium brought it up. Until then, I didn't think there was any other way but for Menou to kill me, and I assumed there was no point trying to go back... But when I think about it now, my leaving this world would still mean Menou survives for longer."

This loop was the first time Pandæmonium had been released. Information from her didn't exist in any of the other time lines.

"Do you *want* to go back?"

"Hmm? No, not particularly. Why would I be happy about returning to a world I barely remember? I'd much prefer to be killed by Menou and live on in her memories... But if it means Menou will live, I figure I'd be fine with going back to Japan."

"...That's really all right with you?"

"Well, yeah, of course it is."

Japan was no longer important to Akari, since she had used up her recollections of it to turn back time when Menou died. Presently, she had more memories of this world than the other.

Momo guessed that her plan was going well.

Akari's memories were clearly deteriorating, nearing total obliteration. She didn't even feel any sense of attachment to her lost recollections. Any that might have been dear to her had been worn away long ago. Akari Tokitou's Pure Concept was bound to lose control soon.

But for some reason, Momo didn't feel happy about it.

She opened her mouth as if to say something but ultimately closed it silently.

That was fine. There were no problems here. Momo

reminded herself that this was all according to plan as she coolly continued the discussion.

"Why did you decide to tell *me* about this? You don't want to go back, right?"

"Because you might be pushy and mean, but you're still a hard worker. It's actually kind of endearing."

"Don't compliment me. That's disgusting."

Momo wrinkled her nose. Seeing this, Akari smiled.

Akari didn't like Momo. She was pushy despite being the younger one, mean-spirited, and had a generally bad attitude. It was so unfair how Menou had a soft spot for her.

But Akari and Momo cared about the same person. On this short journey, she had begun to feel no small amount of sympathy with the other girl.

Consequently, she was starting to think it might be all right if she entrusted things to Momo.

Originally, Akari wanted Menou to be the one to kill her. Her death would mean saving Menou's life, and at the same time, she would remain in Menou's memory forever. Menou definitely wasn't the kind of person who would forget about anyone she slew. Akari wanted to be added to the headstone Menou carved into her own heart.

However...

"I guess I kinda started thinking that my disappearing won't mean Menou is all alone, so maybe a different method wouldn't be so bad," Akari admitted. "If both of you are still around, you can talk about your memories of me, right?"

Momo's mouth moved almost silently.

"Why...are you so...?"

"Hmm? What's up?"

"...Nothing."

Momo's inner conflict slipped in and out of sight. She never finished the line she had almost started to say.

Instead, Momo quickly controlled her expression and casually responded, "All right... I'll think about it, I suppose."

"Yeah? Uh-huh... Cool." Akari stared at Momo intently, making her uncomfortable.

"...What is it?"

"Hmmm? Nothing really."

Momo glared disgustedly at Akari, who was starting to smirk for some reason, but the girl's grin only widened.

"You've never really had friends before, right? You know, since your personality's so awful."

"And so what if I haven't?"

"Hmm? Oh, it's not a big deal. It's just..."

Akari put a hand to her chin and gave a slight cackle. It was obvious at a glance that she was attempting to rile up Momo, which she could only describe as unbelievably irritating.

"Since you don't have a lot of experience dealing with other people, you might be kinda easy to win over, that's all."

"...So you think I'll lose the will to kill you as my darling did? Don't be ridiculous."

"Whaaat? No, I wouldn't go *that* far. But you sure came out with that notion pretty quickly, didn't you, Momo?"

Again, Akari's tone was clearly meant to make Momo feel embarrassed. Momo's fists trembled, but she swallowed back her rage, telling herself it would be giving her enemy precisely what she wanted if she punched her in that stupid face. Instead,

Momo scowled and turned away, as if the very idea was too terrible to discuss.

When she saw this, Akari felt despite herself that she might understand a little bit of why Menou had a soft spot for Momo after all.

Momo was younger than Akari, still only fourteen years old.

"Riiight… She's still in middle school." Realizing this, Akari murmured a quiet regret to herself. "Maybe I went a little overboard with the ribbons…"

Akari had once ruined the ribbons Momo wore in her hair to conveniently force her to move. Incidentally, she was well aware that the ribbons were a gift Momo had received from Menou in their younger days.

While Akari didn't intend for Momo to hear that, she did and froze in place.

"…Ribbons?"

Uh-oh. Akari immediately clamped her hands over her mouth. She'd let slip something that Momo couldn't possibly have figured out otherwise. Momo had changed her hair ties from ribbons to scrunchies in Grisarika Kingdom. Akari should've had no way of knowing about that unless she'd been involved somehow.

To put it another way, the fact that Akari did know about Momo's ribbons was practically a confession that she was connected to the fire that destroyed them.

"Wh…? What did you just say? Something about…ribbons? You went…overboard? What exactly…does that mean?"

Momo's level tone and trailing words were proof that she was barely holding back her rage.

Her keen eyes were full of flaming sparks. They threatened

to burst into an explosion at any moment. Akari had never seen someone so furious in her life.

As Momo trembled with fury, Akari pasted on a forced smile.

"N-nothing at all! It's totally not a big deal or anything, nope. How would I know anything about the red ribbons you used to wear?"

"Why…do you know…about my ribbons?"

Momo saw right through Akari's pathetic attempt at a lie. She grabbed the other girl by the collar and shook her around angrily.

Momo had lost the ribbons Menou gave her during a sequence of events in Grisarika Kingdom, where Akari had been summoned. The assistant Executioner had walked into a trap set by Archbishop Orwell in the old capital of Garm. As she was fighting a dragon-like conjured soldier, something unexpected had occurred.

The barrier protecting her broke with almost unnatural ease.

Incensed at losing the gift from young Menou, Momo went on a rampage and ultimately destroyed a historical building.

"No wonder, no *wonder* the flames got through my barrier…! There's no way that should have happened! I would never fail to protect the ribbons my darling gave me. I knew that wasn't right! You did something, didn't you?!"

"I-I'm sorry, okay?"

Feeling a little guilty at this point, Akari held up her hands in surrender.

Unfortunately, her cheap attempt at an apology did nothing to satisfy Momo.

"Do you…have any idea…how important those were? And

most of all...would *you* forgive the culprit if you were in my position?"

Akari considered the question.

Had someone destroyed the headband that Menou had decorated with a flower for her...would she let the guilty party off the hook with a simple "I'm sorry"?

The verdict was clear.

"...Yeah, I don't think so."

"Exactly."

Without letting go of Akari, Momo used her other hand to lash out with her wirelike coping saw. It was the fastest she'd drawn it in recent memory.

She didn't hit her target, however. The saw only cut through the air and struck the ground.

Momo clicked her tongue with irritation. Akari had vanished instantly, using her Pure Concept of *Time* to teleport. Momo searched for her presence, annoyed that the young woman had gotten so good with her powers.

Behind her, Momo whirled around to see Akari sticking out her tongue, far out of reach.

"Like I'd let you hit me with something so painful-looking. Nyehh, I say!"

Momo's face lost all emotion.

"I'll kill you."

She clenched her fist with an unusually calm expression. Her eyes were full of murderous intent yet stunningly clear.

"I knew that pitying you was a meaningless gesture. Not that I ever felt a shred of it, of course. But just to be clear, I'll say it anyway... *Suffer and die.*"

"Yikes, that's spiteful! Come on, you got those scrunchies you're wearing now, right? You could say that was pretty much thanks to me, timing-wise. If anything, shouldn't you be thanking me?"

"I'm amazed you can spout such drivel so shamelessly! My darling would have given these to me either way. You didn't accomplish that or anything else! Die!"

"It's not fair that you had a memento of the past anyway! It always drove me up a wall how you went around flaunting them in my face!"

"So that's how you really feel!"

Momo didn't care about her plan anymore. She clenched her fist, resolving to kill Akari a hundred times right here and now, forcing her to use up all her memories on *Regression* until she turned into a Human Error on the spot.

Thus began a game of chase that would have looked ridiculous to anyone else but was a severe, deadly fight to the two of them.

What a disgrace.

After Manon and company let her go free, Menou walked toward the inn where Ashuna was waiting, overwhelmed with irritation and anger she couldn't entirely suppress.

It was a complete and utter disgrace. She had failed miserably. These past few days, she'd been utterly worthless as an Executioner.

Manon and Sahara.

Menou had theoretically finished both of them off, yet both had been resurrected in new bodies.

The fact that Manon was traveling with Pandæmonium was

dangerous enough in itself, but she was becoming a foe to be reckoned with in her own right, too.

What's more, there were countless other things to worry about, too.

"The creation of conjurings..."

Menou had some knowledge about conjuring research. Most new ones were developed in a modern technological system. An established conjuring would serve as a basis, and other techniques were derived from it like branches spreading from a tree.

On rare occasions, however, a completely original one would come along that was unmistakably different from any established technique.

There were no facilities for creating unique conjurings anywhere, not even in the holy land.

Still, every few decades, a fresh conjuring was discovered. Where were they coming from?

Menou knew only of one moment when new conjurings came to be.

The Original Sin Concept conjurings.

Original Sin Concepts were born from the wild imagination of one single little girl, scattering her flesh and blood.

The Original Sin Concepts had not existed before Pandæmonium was born.

When the innocent girl with the Pure Concept of *Evil* turned into a Human Error and became Pandæmonium, the Original Sin Concept conjurings were created.

The same was true of the Mechanical Society—the Master of conjured soldiers that operated independently all over and the source of the Concept of Primary Colors that fabricated an entire world. When the Pure Concept of *Vessel* began to go out of control, the system of Primary Colors adhered to this world. Menou knew this all too well because of her extensive studies of materialogy. The only substances that could produce their own Guiding Force without a soul, instead of the user providing Guiding Force to use them, were the Primary Color Stones.

Menou had never pondered too deeply about how unusual these two things were. After all, they were connected to the Four Major Human Errors. Both were strictly considered taboo.

And yet they were undeniably new conjurings.

What kind of world existed in the eastern Wild Frontier? What sort of state was Sahara in? How were the Primary Colors able to create an artificial world and respond to people's wishes? Why were the Four Major Human Errors born simultaneously, leaving massive scars on the planet?

It can't all be connected. Menou's mind tried to reject the hypothesis.

She didn't want to believe that Otherworlders were really victims to that extent and that the Faust was the perpetrator of so much harm.

However, if the theory forming in her mind was true...

The existence of Pure Concepts could be an answer to the fundamental question of the nature of conjurings and related to the meaning of Executioners.

There was only one person Menou knew who might be capable of satisfying those inquiries.

"Once I return to the holy land, I have to ask Master..."

No matter how much she thought about it, Menou couldn't form a solid decision on her own. She was letting herself get too distracted; it was time to calm down.

She took a deep breath. Air filled her lungs and puffed her chest, then she released it slowly.

"...All right."

Menou had reset her mood or at least made her best attempt to do so. Feeling calmer, she was about to return to the inn when she heard voices arguing in an alley.

"I fiiiinally caught you!"

"*Bzzzt!* No, you didn't!"

Both speakers sounded very familiar. Menou froze.

No, surely not. Menou shook her head, confident that she was merely hearing what she wished to. She had come to this town to look for Momo and Akari, but she wasn't even tracking them at the moment.

Running into them on the street was way too improbable. The pair were on the run, after all. Even they should've known better than to draw so much attention to themselves.

Menou felt confident, but just to make sure, she headed for the side street where she'd heard the arguing.

"I really am going to kill you. I can't believe I ever considered showing you a scrap of mercy...!"

"Go ahead and try it, if you think you can! I thought not being able to kill me was the whole problem in the first place, though. Wow, forgetful *and* stupid!"

"ExCUSE me?!"

There could be no denying it now. Momo and Akari were duking it out while shouting at the top of their lungs.

Watching the slightly unbelievable battle unfold in front of her eyes, Menou blinked repeatedly.

This was far too convenient to be happenstance. Perhaps she

was tired? Menou pinched the bridge of her nose, then looked again.

"Even if I can't kill you, there's this lovely little concept called *torture* that I can use to make you suffer! You'll be begging me to end your life by the time I'm through! Maybe I'll start with those unsightly boobs of yours!"

"Momo! It's all over if you give up on your own growth! What if you stay small in all kinds of ways for the rest of your days?!"

"Who said anything about that, you horrible moronnnnnnn!"

Sadly, this was really happening.

The two were so focused on their fight that they hadn't even noticed Menou's presence. The Executioner felt an indescribable exhaustion sink into her soul.

Regardless, she had found them.

"...Momo. Akari."

The two girls froze midcombat.

Momo and Akari turned their heads toward Menou so slowly and mechanically that she could almost hear a metallic creak.

"...What in the world are you two doing?"

Menou had located the two people she was looking for with almost disappointing ease.

An awkward silence filled the air.

In an alley off the main road, unseen by any passersby, three girls were having a very unexpected chance meeting.

Momo, Akari, and Menou. All three knew they were in a game of chase, but not one of them had anticipated it ending in such a foolish way. They had all secretly been imagining, perhaps even hoping, that there would be a more serious pursuit leading to a tense standoff—or something along those lines.

Momo was grinding her teeth in furious regret. She'd been discovered while causing a scene, even if it was only by pure chance.

There was no excuse for her recklessness, and it had never even occurred to her that Menou might already be in the town at this stage of the game. It was far too soon for her to have caught up. Momo was confident she'd had enough time for another two or three days.

Yet Menou was now standing in front of them.

"M-Momo…"

Akari's voice trembled. *Now what?* her gaze asked desperately.

Momo clenched her hand.

Frankly, her desire to punch out the happy-go-lucky girl standing next to her hadn't lessened in the slightest. She wanted to plant her fist right into that obnoxious face. To express all her rage at the culprit who had burned her beloved ribbons.

Still, the assistant Executioner did have a sense of priorities. It would be impossible to deal with Menou while Akari was dragging her down. And even if she did have a Pure Concept, the super good-for-nothing was no match for Menou.

At any rate, Akari needed to be dealt with.

Swallowing her murderous rage, Momo looked around quickly. Within moments, she found an escape route past the walls that enclosed this small alley.

Without a word, Momo enveloped her body in phosphorescent Guiding Light. Menou shot her a wary look, noticing her Guiding Enhancement.

Momo's power wasn't directed at Menou, however. She grabbed Akari with both hands and hissed in her ear.

"I'm going to remove you from my darling's line of sight now—so run for all you're worth."

"Huh?"

Akari blinked in befuddlement. She clearly had no idea what Momo intended.

Unconcerned by her confusion, Momo hefted Akari up in the air. With Guiding Enhancement, a single person's body weight was practically nothing. She held the other girl aloft and shouted, "Fly, you foooooool!"

"Whaaaaa—?!"

As Momo tossed her through the air, Akari could only shriek in surprise.

Her eyes full of tears, Akari soared shockingly high, clearing the hard stone walls that formed the alley and disappearing from view.

"Phew." Momo heaved a sigh of satisfaction and wiped the sweat from her brow. That was an impressive distance. The impact of the landing might kill Akari, but that was no problem. She was immortal. This wouldn't end her life permanently, even if it did traumatize her.

Menou stood there dumbfounded by the sight of a human rocketing into the sky before she came back to her senses with a start and turned her gaze back toward Akari.

"Er, well… I can't say I saw that method of escape coming, but what do *you* plan to do exactly, Momo?"

She was angry. Momo could read Menou's mind from the tone of her voice, and what she detected there sent a shiver down her spine. Even so, she put on her sweetest smile.

"Umm… It's been sooo long, darlingggg. I don't suppose you could give your cute little assistant a pass just this ooooonce?"

"Absolutely not."

"I thought soooo!"

Momo had been hoping Menou would play along a bit more, but instead, she just drew her dagger.

For some reason, Menou seemed more warlike than usual. Momo immediately shifted into battle mode, too.

If she was going to stop her from chasing Akari, she had to buy time. Ideally, she would've liked to do so with conversation, but Menou didn't seem willing to talk.

"I'm a little bit irritated at the moment, you see. If you put up a fight, you're going to get hurt, even if you are my dear assistant."

"Go easy on me! At least go easy on me, pleeease!"

In terms of their overall abilities as Executioners, Menou had the edge over Momo.

But as far as battle skills alone, Momo didn't think she was lesser than Menou by any means.

Her chances of winning were high in close quarters. Even back in the monastery run by their Master, Momo had a higher percentage of wins in hand-to-hand training matches.

The only place she didn't outshine Menou in terms of combat skills was her Guiding Force manipulation.

As Momo tried to lighten the mood, Menou speedily activated a conjuring.

Guiding Force: Connect—Dagger Crest—Invoke [Guiding Thread]

Menou threw her dagger underhand. It was intended more as a feint to limit Momo's movements than to hit its target.

The Guiding Force thread produced from the hilt of the weapon was connected to Menou's hand. Momo jumped forward, trying to catch her before she could pull the dagger back.

Since Menou was trained one-on-one by Master Flare, her conjurings went from construction to invocation with unbelievable speed. She could invoke a crest conjuring in a single breath and even construct and invoke a scripture conjuring within three seconds flat.

Momo almost never used scripture conjurings in combat. She felt that there was no need. Even training under the Master, she'd barely managed to get a passing grade. It wasn't that she couldn't use them at all—it was simply faster to let her Guiding Enhancement and natural strength do the talking, more often than not.

Momo's proficiency in scripture conjurings was mediocre at best, if not worse than the average priestess. It would be the height of folly for her to engage in a scripture conjuring shootout with Menou, who rivaled Master Flare.

Instead, she threw herself forward to maintain the advantage of a close fight, when suddenly—

Guiding Force: Connect—Dagger Crest—Invoke [Gale]

A gust of wind struck her from behind.

"Bwuh?!"

She nearly fell flat on her face but managed to stay upright. Of course, the moment she lost her balance, Menou brought her knee toward Momo's chest.

Momo just barely managed to block with both arms, however.

The impact still knocked her backward. Momo's feet flew

off the ground, and she felt an unpleasant floating sensation in her gut.

"Oh, sh..."

The girl landed an instant later. While she hadn't taken any damage, she had been beaten to the punch. If she let that cow her into submission, the fight was over. Instead, Momo forced a fearless grin, trying to draw the flow of the battle to her side.

"Amazing as always, darliiing. Your dear Momo is no match for youuu. Those were some spectacular moves, but...you said you're irritated? Is something wrooong?"

"All kinds of things. My assistant stole my money in the Balar Desert and ran away. I was forced to play the part of a servant on the way here. I made a serious blunder as soon as I arrived... It's been one stressful situation after another. And so, Momo..."

Menou gave her a bright smile. It was so charming that Momo almost forgot they were in the middle of combat and had to resist the urge to stop and admire her.

"I'd like to resolve the situation with you and Akari right now. Surrender right this instant and explain everything."

"Eh-eh-eh, it's just that we have a liiiittle bit of a situation on our side, toooo. I would love nothing more than to leap into your arms and have you pat my head, but alas, I caaan't..." Momo scratched her cheek sheepishly, avoiding Menou's eyes. "Still, how did you catch up with us so faaast? I thought my chosen route meant you wouldn't be able to catch up without money for suuure..."

"I borrowed some. From Princess Ashuna."

"Whaaat...?"

Her darling, who was always suffering from a lack of funds,

had finally resorted to going into debt. Despite herself, Momo felt a wave of sympathy for her poor Menou.

"Are you all right, darliiing? Borrowing cash is so unsaaafe… If you're in trouble, you should just come to meee! I don't mind financially supporting you at aaall! In fact, I would loooove to!"

"Momo, it was your fault, remember? I wouldn't have had to do this if you hadn't stolen all my funds."

"That's got nothing to do with iiiit. That blasted Princess-poo must've put you through some strange requirements, didn't sheeee?"

"……"

There was no response. Instead, all Menou provided was an expression like she'd sucked on a rotten lemon.

It was all too easy to imagine what that reaction meant. Sensing that her beloved had been defiled in some way, Momo's own expression immediately went blank.

"Excuse me, I'm going to go kill that Princess-poo. She must be at one of the fancier inns in town, I'm sure."

"Wait a minute."

"Don't try to stop meee!"

Murdering Ashuna would allow Momo to dole out some justice and deny Menou her financial support. As always, violence was the answer. The only way to resolve everything was with unconditional brutality, Momo thought as she clenched her fists.

"That accursed Princess-poo deserves nothing but divine punishment for taking advantage of you with all sorts of horrible requests! Plus, you won't have to pay her back if she's dead! It'll work out in your favor, too, darliiing!"

"I told you—wait! It wasn't anything that serious. She just made me dress up as a butler, that's all."

"Dress up as a butler?!"

Menou was trying to appease her with this information, but it had the opposite effect. If anything, Momo heated up even more.

"N-noooo! Why would you let Princess-poo see you in such a rare outfit and not meeee!"

"I'm telling you—it was for money!"

"So if there's cash involved, you'll do a costume change outside of a mission, will yoooou?! Are you willing to do this, that, and the other thing, too, if it's for *in*?! Because if so, I'll go get my life savings for you right nooow!"

"Don't get the wrong idea. Besides, I'm not letting you get away. Why did you think you could escape like that?"

"Tch..."

Momo had tried to flee during the confusion, but a dagger immediately hit the ground in front of her feet. She thought she might have a chance of getting away while their conversation was taking a silly turn, but evidently, that wasn't going to work.

Capture wasn't an option. Momo had no recourse but to fight.

Pulling out her coping saw from within her frilly outfit, Momo flexed the wirelike weapon and wrapped it around her white-gloved hand.

The teeth of the saw were only meant for just that—sawing. They weren't sharp enough to cut into Momo's fist while she was using Guiding Enhancement. She wrapped it around twice to leave no gap between her knuckles and the back of her hand

and lightly wound the rest around her arm so it wouldn't get in the way.

Then she charged it with Guiding Force.

Guiding Force: Connect—Coping Saw Crest—Invoke [Anchor]

The symbol carved into the coping saw responded to Momo's Guiding Force and produced the corresponding effect. The wire wrapped around her fist was reinforced by the *Anchor* conjuring, becoming a simple gauntlet.

If there were any space between them, Menou would immediately use a conjuring. And if mid-to-long-distance combat wasn't an option, this was the only way Momo could use the coping saw. Foolishly moving too far would be inviting a scripture conjuring to put a swift end to the fight.

Seeing that Momo had chosen a fistfight, Menou lashed out with her dagger.

Menou had further reach. If she thrust with her weapon first, Momo's fist wouldn't connect, even if she stretched out her arm.

A dagger could only find purchase at close proximity. Despite being sharply held off, Momo fearlessly stepped closer. She dodged around the blade and moved nearly into punching range.

Guiding Force: Connect—Dagger Crest—Invoke [Gale]

A second crest conjuring. This time, the wind buffeted her head-on.

It was difficult to breathe. The air pressure dried out Momo's eyes. It was almost overly harsh. Piling up many small yet noticeable effects was Menou's go-to method.

The crests inscribed in Menou's dagger were Gale and Guiding Thread. Neither were anywhere near lethal. Menou's

Guiding Force stores were also relatively average, so they weren't strong enough to decide a battle on their own.

However, Menou's strategy didn't rely on the brute strength of her techniques.

All an Executioner needed to do their job was a single fatal stab. Menou's conjurings were only there to help her get the kill. Her varied repertoire was complemented by her ability to use Guiding Camouflage to fool the eye, completing her array of combat arts.

Momo protected her weak points as she opted for the opposite tactic: trying to land a single blow to settle the battle by any means necessary.

She doggedly blocked and dodged Menou's attacks, resigning herself to taking damage as she attempted to entangle her arms.

But just as Momo's hands started to close around Menou's arm, they caught nothing but air.

"What?!"

As she exclaimed wildly, she felt a sharp impact at the base of her skull.

It was an attack from a completely unexpected direction. Stars scattered in her eyes, and her vision went blank as the strength left her body. Momo crumpled to her knees. She managed to get her hands out on the ground before she collapsed completely, primarily out of luck. Using nothing but her sense of touch and arm strength, she forced herself to jump up and away from Menou.

"That...huuurt!"

"...It'd be much more convenient for me if you let that knock you out."

As Momo's vision recovered, she saw Menou standing in front of her, looking inconvenienced indeed.

Momo's eyes filled with tears as the back of her head began to throb in pain, but she stayed conscious through sheer force of will.

She'd been struck in the back of the head with the hilt of Menou's dagger—that much was obvious. The problem was how.

"Dar…ling! When did you get so good at Guiding Camouflage that you can use it while moving like thaaat?!"

"I've been practicing little by little. I have to make constant progress, or my exceptional assistant might surpass me."

Menou had concealed her real arm with Guiding Camouflage and, at the same time, created a feint attack out of Guiding Light. Just two months ago, the best she could manage was blending into her surroundings while standing perfectly still; this was remarkably swift progress.

The attack had been intended as nonfatal, yet Momo barely managed to stay conscious.

She shouldn't have gotten distracted by the use of crest conjurings. Menou was incredibly proficient at drawing her opponent's attention exactly where she wished. She could use her line of sight to attract the eye, throw her dagger as a distraction, and hide with Guiding Camouflage. If she employed all these methods at once, she could spring a surprise attack on someone right in front of her.

Momo was aware of all this in theory, but actually being on the receiving end of it was another story. As she was personally reminded of Menou's strength, she nevertheless couldn't let her darling take her down now. Rather than allowing herself to lose, she decided to buy time by talking.

"Darliiing."

"What is it? You want to surrender? I accept."

"She has memories, you knooow."

Menou was still being kind, so Momo tossed out a piece of information she couldn't ignore.

Sure enough, Menou took the bait.

"Memories?"

"Akari Tokitou, that is. She has been turning back time, just like you thought. And what's more, she was hiding the fact that she retains her memories from each instance."

Menou faltered.

It utterly infuriated Momo that her beloved Menou would be rattled by news about Akari, but she couldn't be choosy about her methods if she hoped to succeed.

"She knew how the journey was going to go."

"...I see."

Menou exhaled quietly.

She didn't seem overly troubled. Most likely, she already knew this was a possibility. Momo and Menou had already discussed the theory that Akari might be rewinding time on a large scale.

During their talk, they'd guessed that Akari's memories were reset, too, aside from perhaps a vague sense of familiarity. That had been wrong.

"So you decided to take drastic action to change the future forcibly."

"Yes."

"Very well. I admit that I was at fault, as well. But I do think you ought to have discussed things with me first. The position of an assistant priestess is not so casual that you possess total discretionary power."

"But there are things we can't tell yoooou."

Telling Menou ruined everything. It was paramount that she was not aware of what would transpire.

If nothing changed, Menou was going to die.

Akari kept spending her memories to turn back time in order to save her.

Momo didn't want Menou to know the depth of Akari's devotion. It wasn't just for emotional reasons; she was afraid of what kind of changes that might cause to Menou's state of mind.

Discovery might very well lead to Menou deciding to save Akari.

When Momo stated that she knew what the future held, Menou's eyes narrowed.

"Momo. What's going to happen?" she asked sharply.

"It's a secreeet."

"I see. I had a feeling you might say that."

Momo readied herself. In exchange for giving up a small amount of information, she had bought enough time for her mind to recover from the blow.

"Momo. Would you please surrender already? I'll have to punish you for acting without permission, but if you've gotten valuable information out of Akari, I'm willing to be lenient."

She probably meant she would let it slide with that as an excuse. Momo was classified as a priestess and an Executioner, but only an assistant one. Disobeying her superior's orders was worthy of severe discipline.

"On the other hand, if you refuse to stop, you do realize you'll be in for a world of pain, right?"

"Any pain inflicted by my darling would be my plea-surrrre... But! I'm afraid, it'll have to wait for a liiittle longer, pleeease!"

As they spoke, Momo searched for an escape route.

She had underestimated the difference between Menou's and her own abilities. Clearly, she was wrong to think she had a chance of winning, even in close combat. Fleeing was the only choice.

They hadn't solved anything yet.

Momo wouldn't back down as long as Menou's life was on the line. She couldn't let her darling find Akari. Momo refused to compromise, even if it meant sacrificing her position.

Her goal was to hold out until Menou had to give up on Akari.

Could they get away? Momo winced at the question.

It would be tough. Fleeing on her own was one thing. After-ward, she could recover Akari, get on a train, and abscond. Unfortunately, it was far too optimistic to assume everything would go without a hitch.

It might even be delusional, Momo mused with a grim smile.

Still, she had to succeed.

Seeing that Momo was unwilling to back down, Menou's eyes hardened. Her focused determination to win at all costs prickled at Momo's skin.

Just as the battle was about to resume, a voice cut in.

"That's enough," declared a cool voice. An enormous sword was suddenly thrust between the two young women.

*   *   *

Akari was lucky not to die after Momo hurled her into the air.

Just before she started falling, her clothes caught on a duct attached to a wall, slowing her down significantly. The vent in question was damaged in the process, and while she felt guilty about that, she managed to get away without causing a fuss.

Now that Akari was out of Menou's sight, she started running as quickly as she could, just as Momo told her.

"Momo… She's actually really stupid, isn't she…?"

Akari was hardly overflowing with gratitude. Really, how thankful could she be for the act of tossing her over a wall? Grumbling to herself about Momo's violent and absurd nature, Akari kept moving.

Then, after ten minutes of walking, Akari stopped and looked up at the sky.

"Where am I…?"

She was lost.

Akari had ended up on the outskirts of town, on an even more obscure side street. Momo would undoubtedly curse her out at great length if she knew about this, but Akari felt it wasn't fair to blame her entirely. After all, she had never been to this village before. On top of that, Akari had been avoiding main roads to stay out of sight since Menou might be pursuing her.

It didn't help that being tossed into the air was utterly disorienting. Put it all together, and Akari was as remarkably lost as any child separated from her parents.

"What should I do now…?"

Gazing at the sky, where the sun was beginning to set, Akari folded her arms and thought hard.

She and Momo had agreed on an emergency meeting place just in case they got separated. It was the train station one town over from this one.

As such, Akari should have been heading for the train station, yet she hadn't the faintest idea how to get there. She was standing contemplating the problem with an obviously ditzy expression on her face when a voice called out to her.

"Hey, whassamatter, little lady? You in trouble?"

A group of boorish-looking boys blocked the alley behind her.

There were three of them in total, all of whom could only be described as common hoodlums. Akari had evidently wandered into an area frequented by the local delinquents.

"…Who are you?"

"Ha-ha, ain't no reason for us to tell you that."

"Although, I guess I'd tell ya my name if ya spend the night with me tonight."

The young men snickered as they drew closer.

Based on appearances alone, Akari did seem like an easy mark. She didn't look strong at all, and what's more, her tidy outfit helped give her the appearance of an innocent, well-to-do young lady. Standing around in an empty alley like this was bound to attract the wrong kind of attention.

They looked around the same age, but any ordinary girl would likely be trembling with fear if such ruffians approached her. They steadily closed in, hinting that they weren't going to take no for an answer.

Akari wasn't frightened in the least, however.

Thanks to Momo dragging her around over the past few

days, she'd gotten distressingly accustomed to combat. These delinquents were nowhere near the already low-level criminals she and Momo had been beating up recently.

Talking to them didn't even seem worth the bother. Akari was pointing her finger at them like a gun, intending to use *Suspension* to turn them into statues for the next half day or so (a violent thought that showed Momo had clearly influenced her), when she was interrupted by a voice.

"Hmm, I recognize this girl. I'll have to make sure you don't lay a hand on her, then."

"Hunh? Who the h—? Aargh?!"

Someone new entered the alley and sent one of the boys flying with a magnificent punch.

His friends opened their mouths to protest furiously, but they swallowed their words in terror when they beheld the intruder.

They'd been interrupted by a tall woman whose blond hair had hints of red.

She gave off an air that was worlds apart from Akari's. While her outfit exposed a lot of skin, her remarkable figure was more likely to inspire admiration than lust. It was clear from the sword she carried that she was a knight, but even without the huge sword in her hand, it was apparent at a glance that it would be a bad idea to cross her. The boys fled without even a parting word.

"Well, hello again."

Akari recognized her rescuer, too.

They had only met a single time, and both had been wearing swimsuits, which had left a strong impression.

"You're, umm…"

"Ashuna Grisarika. You are Akari Tokitou, correct?"

She reintroduced herself, looking unbothered that Akari couldn't immediately recall her name, and continued with a question.

"What are you doing in a place like this? This might be a tourist town, but it still isn't safe for someone to go wandering in the alleys alone."

"Er... I sort of got lost." Akari scratched her cheek sheepishly, then figured she might as well make the best of the situation, turning on her puppy-dog eyes. "I don't suppose you could guide me to the station as a..."

Just as she was making the request, her stomach suddenly growled loudly.

Akari instinctively pressed her hands to her stomach, her face turning bright red with embarrassment. Ashuna gave her a charming grin.

"I'll be happy to guide you, but...shall we share a bite to eat first?"

Her cheeks still flushed crimson, Akari nodded without another word.

✳✳✳

"Thanks for the food!"

Akari pressed her hands together, offering her heartfelt thanks to the ingredients that had been on her now-cleaned plate, the chef that made the dish, and most of all, the person who had treated her to the meal.

Sitting across from her, Ashuna gave a generous nod.

"You're a hearty eater."

The pair were in a restaurant on the main road. Ashuna had

brought Akari to an arbitrarily chosen establishment with a curtained entrance.

"I really appreciate it. I missed out on lunch because Momo was chasing me around."

"Don't worry about it. This is no trouble at all for me. More importantly, let's hear the rest of your story."

"Sure! Momo is just so mean, you know?"

At Ashuna's invitation, Akari was happy to continue rambling.

Apparently, Ashuna knew that Akari was a lost lamb. She also had a rough idea of the Faust's situation and asked Akari to tell her about her time with Momo.

Now that she had calmed down, perhaps a bit too much, Akari was happy to talk about her time in this town. Once she described the events from their quest to purge criminals to the chase between her and Momo, Ashuna smirked.

"Hrmm. I suspected as much, but I do pity poor Menou. And Momo is an impulsive fool as usual... Still, a method of returning to the other world, hmm?"

"Momo is one thing, but there's nothing pitiful about Menou! ...Wait a minute, Ms. Ashuna. Do you know something about that?"

Ashuna Grisarika. Hearing her family name made it clear that she had some connection to the Grisarika Kingdom that had summoned Akari.

Ashuna had stated during their conversation that she wasn't involved in the summoning, but Akari still gave her a hopeful look.

"We can discuss that later."

"Later?"

"Yes. Now's not the time."

Ashuna avoided the topic with a chilly, grim smile that was unlike her usual showy grin.

"But know this, Akari Tokitou."

"Huh?"

"How did you lost ones begin appearing in this world? There isn't a single person who knows the answer, and we have no way of knowing. There is research that suggests that there were no Otherworlders before the rise of the ancient civilization, but...unfortunately, the scars left by the Four Major Human Errors are too deep to make much of an attempt at retracing the threads of history."

"Oh..." Akari blinked in confusion as Ashuna used her full name and brought up an unexpected subject. "Really?"

"Indeed. And perhaps there was never a reason for the arrival of Otherworlders to begin with. Yet this world is remarkably harsh to your kind. And so the same events repeat over and over. It's not just your problem alone. There's no right or wrong answer."

Her words strangely convincing, Ashuna pointed a finger at Akari's chest.

"Understand that it is exactly why the Faust continues to create Executioners."

What did she mean by all this? Akari tilted her head at the strange, one-sided conversation.

Fully aware that Akari wouldn't yet comprehend, the other woman smiled boldly.

"Now, that was enough of a break, don't you agree? Let's go to the station, as you requested."

For her, this next part was what she truly sought.

*　　*　　*

The large sword that cleaved through the air and cut between them prompted Momo and Menou to freeze.

Ashuna stepped in, having stopped their fight by throwing her broadsword between the pair.

"How kind of you to leave me behind."

The veins popping on her temple indicated her impressively sour mood. Ashuna's rage was so palpable that it filled the air and prickled the skin.

This was unusual for Ashuna, who was born into a royal Noblesse family and carried herself with a proud and open-handed air accordingly. What had made her so furious? Menou and Momo were both at a loss.

"Especially you, Menou. I should have expected no less. You played the part of a solemn servant perfectly, but you were secretly waiting to betray me, I see. How many years has it been since I was last drugged without my knowledge, I wonder...?!"

"Excuse me?"

"And then you went and took my belongings, too... I knew you didn't have any money, but I never imagined you would stoop to petty theft. I thought you were honorable by nature, but evidently, my assessment was wrong. Would you care to explain yourself? Go on; I'm listening."

Menou gaped in bewilderment. Momo was looking at her with a sparkling expression that said something like, *You poisoned Princess-poo, robbed her blind, and abandoned her? You're so incredible, darling!* However, Menou had done no such thing. She genuinely had no idea what Ashuna was going on about.

Ashuna had accompanied Menou to the inn once she secured lodging there. It was true that Menou had carried her

©nilitsu

bags, but that hardly qualified as thievery. She left the luggage in their room at the inn.

"Your Highness. Er… I truly do not understand. What in the world are you saying?"

"Oh-ho?"

Ashuna's answer was short and sharp.

She strode over and retrieved her broadsword from where it was stuck in the ground.

Then she gave the blade a swing, whistling through the air. Her eyes narrowed as she leveled it straight at Menou.

"Playing dumb is hardly an exciting response. If that's the best excuse you can come up with, perhaps I'll have you pay me back in blood?"

Ashuna's anger was unmistakably genuine as she readied her beloved weapon. The broadsword she always carried was a Guiding vessel engraved with several crests. It certainly wasn't the kind of thing you pointed at a person in jest.

Menou's confusion deepened. She had been accused of robbery and poisoning but had no recollection of doing either. It sounded almost as if Ashuna had interacted with Menou when Menou wasn't actually there. That meant that the Ashuna Menou had brought to the inn wasn't really Ashuna at all.

Had Ashuna just misunderstood something? Menou's brow furrowed. Her story didn't make any sense unless both Menou and Ashuna had look-alikes.

But that was impossible. Unless…

She knew of a single person who could do such a thing.

"……!"

Momo and Menou both solved the mystery at the same time. They both gasped and looked at each other.

"Please describe everything that happened…!"

Abandoning the fight, Menou rushed over to Ashuna to get all the details.

Ashuna led Akari safely to the station.

Akari sighed in relief at the familiar sight.

"Should you be leaving alone? Aren't you here with Momo?"

"We agreed beforehand to meet at the station in the next town over if anything happened."

Their meeting place was in a different station instead of the inn where they were staying because they'd been going around defeating criminals.

The idea was that if they were attacked in retaliation and could no longer stay in town, and Momo and Akari got unexpectedly separated, they could prioritize leaving town at once while still meeting up again.

"I see. That means you're taking the same train I am, then."

"Oh, really?" Akari responded absently, not particularly suspicious. "What a coincidence."

This wasn't the pair's first encounter. They'd met briefly at the oasis before traveling to the western part of the continent, though they barely spoke at the time. Ashuna was a very distinctive individual, one that was hard to forget.

At the same time…

Out of the many instances Akari had repeated this journey, this was the first time she'd met Ashuna.

"Ms. Ashuna, you're a princess, right? Why are you traveling like this?"

"Hmm? Ah, I see. So this is the first time."

What does she mean by that? The first what? Akari gazed at

Ashuna's lovely features as she pondered the meaning of the woman's words.

"The eldest daughter of Grisarika Kingdom must have determined that this time is the last. And so I, Ashuna Grisarika, left the kingdom."

"Uh-huh…"

Just as she had when they shared a meal, Ashuna spoke of very esoteric things. She seemed self-centered, as if she had no intention of Akari understanding the meaning behind her statements. Unable to do anything but agree, Akari followed her into the station.

"Look, there's our train."

The locomotive on the furthest platform was a very luxurious-looking one.

Akari's eyes widened. It was a short train with only five cars, but the design was very holy-looking. Even Akari could tell that this was special.

"This is my personal conveyance. I can have it prioritized over any other schedule to take it wherever I want."

"Whaaat?!"

Only a princess could prepare such a remarkable thing. She exclaimed with awe as she entered the car, stepping onto plush red carpeting. A little startled by the sinking sensation, Akari nonetheless continued inside, her eyes widening when she realized the entire car was one big, luxurious room.

"All right, this is—hrmm?"

There were two passengers already on the train. Judging by the scowl on Ashuna's face, she hadn't been expecting them.

"I don't recall inviting either of you…," she growled.

One was an unfamiliar man. He was well-dressed in a suit

and bowler hat and appeared to be in his fifties. The spitting image of an upper-class gentleman, he looked perfectly at home in the elegant surroundings.

While Akari had never seen him before, the girl sitting across from him was unmistakable.

Pandæmonium, a little girl more terrifying than any demon, was waiting for Akari on a sofa.

What was she doing here? Before Akari could even question it, she was already pointing her index finger at the girl.

It was a primarily instinctive reaction. That was how much she feared the childlike monster. Ignoring Ashuna's indignant voice, Akari let Guiding Light shine around her fingertip.

Guiding Force: Connect—Improper Attachment, Pure Concept [Time]—

She was about to use *Suspension*, a conjuring she had used so often that it came nearly as naturally as *Regression*.

The construction assembled within a second, and she was about to invoke it when suddenly—

"Stop."

"...Nngh?!"

Her finger was broken.

It was Ashuna who did it. Right as Akari took aim, she'd reached out, grabbed the girl's finger, and broken it without a moment's hesitation.

Akari's conjuring fell apart and vanished. The fact that her Pure Concept was attached to her soul meant she could effortlessly use conjurings, but it also meant she couldn't consciously maintain the constructions.

"Why...did you...?!"

"In most cases…"

Why had she attacked Akari? As the red-hot shock faded, the wave of pain sent Akari into a cold sweat.

Ashuna watched the young woman clutch her broken finger in agony and continued to speak casually.

"Most Otherworlders, who are untrained and use conjurings unconsciously, develop some kind of bad habit when they construct or invoke conjurings. In your case, you use your index finger to point at the target. Tell Momo that if she's claiming to train you, she could at least teach you to fix that much."

Akari *did* tend to point her finger like a gun when she used a conjuring. It was easier for her to have a corresponding action for invoking a conjuring to solidify her aim.

However, it also left her open to attack.

"Your attacks aren't a threat in the least. It's child's play to dodge a conjuring when you know exactly where and when it's coming. The only remaining problem is that you refuse to die."

Even as she trembled in pain, Akari used *Regression* on her broken finger to heal it. She tried to explain to Ashuna that she'd made a massive mistake by stopping her attack.

"That's not… What I mean is… Why did you stop me…? That's no ordinary kid!"

"I'm aware."

Ashuna nodded coolly, and her outline wavered. For a moment, Akari didn't quite understand what was happening. Then she recalled witnessing this phenomenon somewhere before.

"Wha…?"

As Akari realized what was going on, her face blanched.

She felt the same sort of fear that Archbishop Orwell had during the battle in Grisarika Kingdom.

Near the end of the fight below the cathedral, when Orwell saw that Menou had used Guiding Camouflage to disguise herself, she had been astonished and despondent. Akari was no different now.

"I'm well aware of how dangerous Pandæmonium is without cautioning from the likes of you."

There was no hesitation in her response, suggesting that she was used to seeing people react to her this way. She hooked her fingertips under Akari's chin and lifted her face.

Her mannerisms and speech no longer resembled Ashuna's at all.

The disguise of Ashuna Grisarika melted away.

An aggressively skimpy outfit turned into the formal dark-blue robes of a priestess. Long blond hair became short and dark red. Her youthful, confident face turned into one that had seen too much in the line of duty and regarded the world with cynicism.

Guiding Camouflage.

It was a precise form of Guiding Force manipulation that fooled the eyes of others. This ability wasn't flashy and had no capacity for bodily harm. If anything, it was a mastery of avoiding attention.

Menou, also known as Flare's successor, Flarette, had used this technique as a trump card, and there was only one person more proficient at it than her.

Akari could only gawk speechlessly at the woman who had used her unshakable spirit to disguise herself for so long.

"We have unexpected guests, but...oh well." She glanced

at the other two passengers, then back at Akari, and openly laughed. "Let's have a little chat, shall we, Akari Tokitou?"

This was the Executioner who had hunted the most taboos in history, consequently becoming a living legend.

Master Flare had revealed herself before Akari.

©nilitsu

CHAPTER 5

And Thus the Chase Begins

Menou and company had returned to their room in the inn.

After meeting up in the alley, the trio decided it would be best to go someplace where they could calm down and compare their sides of the story.

"So let me get this straight…" Ashuna's anger was slowly shifting to doubt as Menou explained the situation. "When we first arrived at the station here, the person who gave me tea in the rest area wasn't really you. The scoundrel who put sleeping powder in my drink just happened to look exactly like you. But you say you have no recollection of those events, Menou?"

"Not at all. And just to confirm, the person who entered the inn with me wasn't really you, either, Your Highness?"

"Damn right it wasn't."

Menou clearly recalled Ashuna handing her the luggage and walking to the inn with her. Yet Ashuna denied any memory of that happening.

"Since you were playing the part of my servant at the time,

I would never have gone out to greet you. From my perspective, it seemed clear that you had drugged my tea and ran off with my belongings."

Ashuna rested her hand on her fist, making her look even more irritable.

"I was knocked out in that rest area. It was far too unnatural to be anything except a drug. Timing-wise, it must have been in the tea that false Menou gave me. I do have a high tolerance, so...it must have been something powerful."

Ashuna didn't bother hiding her scowl upon realizing she had been duped.

"So there are fakes of both of us. Who's behind this?"

No one objected to her conclusion about the discrepancy. Menou felt the same way as the princess. Someone had flawlessly impersonated both of them.

"I do have one idea."

"This was no mere disguise with costumes or makeup. It was impeccable. What is this fake hoping to achieve? Perhaps they hoped to cause a falling-out between us?"

"No... I don't think so."

Menou shook her head.

It took precision to replace both of them with such flawless timing. Given the way it was executed, only one person could've been responsible.

Master Flare.

It was an extraordinary feat to become two different people, determine the nature of their relationship, and fool them both, all without any preparation. Only the legendary Executioner who could alter her appearance perfectly with Guiding Camouflage had a hope of succeeding.

"Darling...," Momo called as she approached. While Menou and Ashuna discussed things, the apprentice priest- ess had checked the inn where she and Akari were staying to look for the Otherworlder. Ignoring Ashuna as naturally as she breathed, Momo reported directly to Menou. "Akari Tokitou hasn't returned to the inn."

"...I see."

That settled it.

Menou and Momo had both lost track of Akari.

Abducting her was surely Master Flare's objective, then.

"I'm going to find out what's going on."

"Please, don't go."

If Master Flare planned to spirit Akari away, she would defi- nitely take her to the station. No sooner did Menou come to that conclusion than she moved to stand, but Momo stopped her.

"Momo?"

"This is for the best."

Momo held on to one sleeve of Menou's priestess robes. For some reason, it sounded like she was trying to convince herself more than her beloved superior.

"It's better this way, riiight? We can just let Master take care of everything."

"How is this better? It's far too sudden, even for Master. And I don't even understand why. Surely I have the right to protest, at the very—"

"You're the reason Akari Tokitou was turning back time, darling." As Menou insisted that she had to know her Master's motives, Momo revealed the truth they'd been hiding all this time. "She wanted to save you before you betray the Faust for her sake...and to change the future in which Master Flare kills you for that betrayal. So she rewound the entire world. Many times, in fact."

"...What?"

Menou's first reaction to Momo's words was bewilderment.

Akari had been using *Regression* to repeat the same period, which was astonishing on its own, but the reason baffled Menou more.

"I forsake...the Faust?"

"Yes."

"I turn traitor to save Akari?"

"Yes."

"And then Master kills me—Akari said all this?"

"Yes."

Momo nodded once for each question.

Menou, an Executioner, would turn her back on the Faust to save Akari's life and be killed by her Master.

Akari had been turning back time over and over to avoid that outcome.

Even after hearing it, it didn't seem real.

At this point, Menou couldn't deny that she felt friendship toward Akari. But she was raised as an Executioner and knew all too well the dangers of Otherworlders. She couldn't imagine throwing all that away to try to save Akari.

That motive seemed at odds with Menou's behavioral principles.

"Darling... Could you kill Akari Tokitou right now? It doesn't have to be with the Sword of Salt. Could you stab her with the dagger at your thigh, even if she would come back?"

"Obviously, I cou—"

"That's easier said than done."

Why wouldn't she be able to?

"I'm quite sure you couldn't. The fact that Master is here now is proof enough, isn't it?"

Master Flare would undoubtedly succeed at slaying Akari. There was no doubt. She was capable of everything Menou was and more.

Still, nothing was keeping Menou from ending Akari's life. Manon said something along similar lines in their exchange, but Menou wasn't that weak. Of course she wasn't.

She knew her way of life better than anyone else.

Yet Momo kept arguing desperately. "Darling, you're alive. Master came, Akari is gone, and you're still alive and well. What could matter more than that?" Momo seemed to read something in Menou's silence. She hesitated, as if unsure whether to say something else, then quietly added, "It's what she wanted, too."

These words, which Momo said to convince Menou, were likely her biggest mistake.

Akari wanted to sacrifice herself to save Menou.

Menou's refusal to accept the future Momo described suddenly inverted upon hearing as much.

"...Ah, I see now."

Now Menou understood why a version of her in another time loop would do something so contradictory to her thought process. Her heart settled into where it was meant to be with a dull thud.

"So that's how it happens."

A small, self-derisive laugh escaped Menou's lips.

"Sorry, Momo. I'm still going to go see Master for a bit."

"N-no, you can't. You'll die, darling! Don't you realize that's a real possibility?!"

"It's always a possibility. I'm an Executioner, after all. There's always the risk that I might die."

"That's not the issue here!"

"Yes, it is."

Menou gave a fleeting smile. She stood up and stretched. After some casual warm-up exercises, she took her leave.

"Darling!"

"I almost died not long ago, you know," Menou responded quite casually to Momo's plea.

"What?" Momo's mouth fell open. Without replying directly, Menou reflected on her recent near-death experience.

In the battle in the desert, Menou was defeated and nearly died.

"When I was about to perish, I realized I didn't want to."

That was probably the first time in Menou's life that she'd felt that way.

She had come close to death before. In the short while since meeting Akari, she'd fought Pandæmonium and been cornered by Orwell. During both instances, she could've met her demise at any moment.

But that time in the desert was when she first thought she didn't want to die.

"I pictured you and Akari, and I thought, *I really don't want to let it end here.*"

Menou reached out her hand to her assistant's pink hair. She touched the base of each pigtail, patting her head. Her eyes softened when she saw that Momo was wearing the scrunchies she'd given her, then she went on.

"So I won't. I'll come back alive."

Momo bit her lip. She began to speak, but she had to give up when she looked directly into Menou's face.

There was no talking the other girl out of it. Instead, she looked up at her for a promise.

"You aren't lying, are you?"

"I've never once lied to you, right, Momo?"

Momo thought it over carefully. She searched her memories and failed to come up with a single instance of Menou lying to her. So she gave a slight nod.

"Then trust me."

Menou was hardly planning to go to her death.

At least, not today.

"I'm just going to have a little conversation with Master, that's all. You wait here with Princess Ashuna."

Menou left the inn with her usual strides, leaving Momo behind.

The sunset was beginning to dye the sky in golden hues. Menou's shadow stretched long on the main road. She moved as if chasing her shadow, first at a steady walk, then quickening her pace, until finally, she broke into a run.

"Stop being ridiculous, stupid Akari."

Muttering darkly, Menou ran toward the girl she was grumbling about.

Tinted sunlight streamed through the enormous train window. The sun was beginning to set, its golden light gradually reddening as it illuminated the land.

Four people were gathered in the train car.

A priestess with dark-red hair was sitting across from Akari.

Master Flare had disguised herself as Ashuna and managed to lead Akari here and capture her without the slightest suspicion.

There were also two uninvited guests aboard.

"And here I thought I'd taken care of things with minimal effort, only to be bothered by a pair of interlopers... So this is what they mean by forgetting the finishing touches."

Flare's eyes narrowed in annoyance as she glared at the pair.

One of the guests was a young girl.

Pandæmonium—a cherubic little girl with black hair and black eyes. She could appear anywhere at any moment, and right now, she looked for all the world like a child caught in the act of an innocuous prank.

The other intruder was a man in his late fifties. As Flare glowered at him, he doffed his bowler hat in apology.

"I am truly sorry. I was simply too eager to speak with you after so long."

"Well, I wasn't expecting ever to see you again. You should've just holed up for the rest of your life, but I guess you couldn't handle that."

"Indeed, perhaps you are right. Unlike me after years in prison, you have scarcely aged at all. I am rather jealous, Flare. So whose pawn have you become now, I wonder?"

"Is that all you came here to ask? Well, go ahead and laugh. The Magician."

"Oh-ho, dear me!" His dubious-looking expression turned sympathetic. "I do pity you that. What an absolutely pointless waste of space that person is."

"Agreed. Not that there are any good Elders in the bunch."

They exchanged words as if in casual conversation. The Director cast a glance toward Akari.

"And? What do you plan to do once you bring her to the holy land?"

"Make her lose control."

Akari's shoulders trembled at the direct response.

"I'll take her to the land of salt, make her turn into a Human Error, and dispose of her. Just like that other time."

"But why…?"

Akari interrupted before she could stop herself.

Flare had just said she was going to make her lose control, not execute her.

It didn't make sense. Wasn't the entire point of Executioners to prevent Pure Concepts from going out of control?

"Young lady. That answer is deeply connected to the question of how conjurings are created. Otherworlders have been brought here many times over the years, whether by arbitrary summoning or natural phenomena, but you are one of few who—ah, pardon me."

The Director ceased his lengthy rambling when he noticed Flare scowling at him.

"Akari Tokitou. You've been kept alive because your concept was deemed worthy of being written in the scriptures."

The Master took over from the Director to give a short response, but Akari didn't understand. Master Flare, who had no intention of explaining it to her in the first place, gave an icy smile.

"Incidentally, I've heard you're searching for a way back to the other world. I assume Pandæmonium here told you about that? What a pleasant thought."

Upon the mention of returning to the other world, the Director's expression turned to something like pity.

Unlike him, Pandæmonium was almost disturbingly quiet. She simply listened to the conversation with a fixed smile.

"There is a theory regarding a conjuring to send Otherworlders back. Shall I explain it to you?"

"You know it...?"

"Sure."

As Akari's voice trembled, the Master threw back her head and laughed.

"You would have to suck up enough Guiding Force to be on par with all the astral veins on the continent, draw a conjuring circle with a large nation's worth of materials, offer about a third of the world's population as sacrifices, and then if anyone was capable of controlling the resulting conjuring, theoretically you should be able to send someone from this world to the other one."

"...Huh?"

Akari's mind refused to process the information.

Even without understanding conjurings, she comprehended that this was a ridiculous pipe dream. It would be all but impossible to put such a ritual into practice. It was theoretically possible, but nothing more. Anyone who genuinely suggested an attempt would be seen as senseless.

And yet Master Flare was describing it in perfect seriousness.

"That is what the Four Major Human Errors attempted to do."

Akari's attention automatically shifted to Pandæmonium as Flare went on.

"It does seem wild, but it's actually very impressive.

Apparently, they really did come close to succeeding a thousand years ago. They miraculously managed to have Pure Concepts powerful enough, and they all had a strong desire to go back home. *Dragon* gathered Guiding Force in the west, *Vessel* collected materials in the east, *Evil* assembled sacrifices in the south, and *Star* constructed the conjuring circle in the north. Whether it was right or wrong, they were almost able to open the gate back to their home world. And would you believe it?"

Flare's cynical gaze pierced through Akari, who came from the same place as the Four Major Human Errors.

"They did it while they were still sane, before they became Human Errors."

Most people who knew of the Four Major Human Errors had a fundamental misconception about them.

The quartet of Otherworlders who wrought catastrophic damage across the continent didn't cause most of their harm after their Pure Concepts went out of control. They used their Pure Concepts of their own free will to wreak calamities on the planet.

"That's the real reason we see you Otherworlders as our enemies. And you'll be pleased to hear this. There's a system for retaining the memories of Otherworlders who have used their Pure Concepts, too."

Master Flare smirked contemptuously as she revealed the truth behind the horrible events of a thousand years ago.

"After all, it's because they were able to supplement their memories that the Four Major Human Errors were able to cause far more damage than by simply letting their Pure Concepts go out of control."

The Otherworlders who had learned of a method to return

home made their attempt with no regard for the sacrifices required. Once a battle broke out with the powers that tried to stop them, they cut the wounds that would continue to ravage each part of the continent for a thousand years.

Thanks to their ability to preserve their memories, they could use their Pure Concepts with almost no risk involved, resulting mass destruction. In the midst of the turmoil, the only two who survived were the Mechanical Society and Pandæmonium, who became Human Errors that couldn't be killed entirely.

It didn't matter that there was a system that could prevent Otherworlders from losing control.

In the era of the ancient civilization that possessed a system to keep Otherworlders from running berserk, the Four Human Errors still devastated the world. Their Pure Concepts weren't out of control. It was their own will and fury with which they brought ruin.

That was why Otherworlders were dangerous.

"You all cause nothing but harm. To the point where we can't tolerate any so-called exceptions."

The existence of Otherworlders who wished to go back to their world so desperately that they were willing to slaughter as many people as it took brought an end to an entire civilization. After a tragedy on that scale, this land could no long tolerate a system that permitted people with Pure Concepts to exist.

Akari couldn't say a word.

Her eyes remained trained on the little girl with black hair. The evening sun shone onto her dress with holes in the chest, dying it a beautiful crimson.

"…You tricked me."

She'd been told that a way back existed and had held on to that tiny bit of hope.

In her conversation with Momo, Akari had voiced the idea that maybe, instead of her death, the journey could end with a sad farewell.

But it wasn't possible.

Such a conclusion could never exist for her.

"Mmm?"

Akari would've preferred not to know. She stared at Pandæmonium bitterly, and the child rested her chin in her hands.

"That wasn't my intent. I didn't lie once, you know. I really wasn't even trying to deceive you. I mean, it does exist, doesn't it?"

Pandæmonium leaned back in the seat of the train car, her legs not even reaching the floor, and turned her nose up with a prim huff.

"*...There was a way to return...*" to Japan.

She was the one who told Akari that.

"Mm, maybe I neglected to mention that you'd need sacrifices, but it shouldn't be that hard to figure that out. We tried to destroy the world because we needed them, after all."

The Four Human Errors had consumed all the southern islands to offer up a vast amount of human lives, took over the eastern part of the continent to gather a nation's worth of land for materials, went to the western part of the continent to acquire mass quantities of Guiding Force, and concentrated all this in the north of the continent to start preparing the conjuring to send them back to the other world. Ultimately, they lost *Ivory*, the strongest Pure Concept of all.

"I'm not sure why you seem so sad about this. Didn't you

say you didn't need a way back? You were so convinced that your friendship meant you'd be content to die in this world... Mmm, oh, I know!"

The girl clapped her hands to her mouth in an overdramatic display of surprise.

"Could it be that you've started wanting to survive after all?"

Pandæmonium's lips curled up in a wicked grin.

"I guess that makes sense. There's nothing wrong with a change of heart. You're human. You thought you were okay with dying, but then you start to think maybe you keep living. That's a wonderful kind of friendship! In a movie, that'd be the scene where you get excited over a path to a happy ending. The hope that you can return to your own world. The expectation that everything will fall into place if you just try. Honestly, why the long face?"

Looking delighted, Pandæmonium gave a little giggle. She drew close to Akari as she went on.

"Don't tell me you think the method you just learned about sounds hard? Well, not to worry. It's not going to be difficult at all. I should know!"

She leaned over to whisper in Akari's ear like she was telling her a secret.

"The Mechanical Society is still turning the east into Primary Color materials even as we speak. For the Guiding Force, *Dragon*'s legacy has gathered all the earthen veins of the continent in the holy land. The conjuring circle that *Star* built yet remains in the north. And you can leave the sacrifices to me, okay?"

Pandæmonium's every word was sincere. She was incapable of lying.

Moving away from Akari, Pandæmonium spread her arms wide.

"Mm-mm, how lucky you are! Everything you need is still left perfectly intact!"

Her voice was syrupy sweet, enough to rot one's heart from the inside out.

Flare and the Director watched Pandæmonium's monologue in silence. A concept with the ability to destroy the world was bidding Akari join her, but the pair simply observed without interrupting.

"Don't you get it? If you use this whole continent, the gate to the other world will open. All your wishes will come true. Nothing is impossible if you try! A wonderful happy ending where both you and your beloved friend get to live is waiting for you!"

The red-tinged sunlight flooded in through the window. Twilight was descending on the train car.

With her dress colored a bloody hue, Pandæmonium made a frame with her two index fingers and thumbs and held it up to one eye.

"You would risk your life for the one you care about. You would even destroy the whole world."

Admiring Akari through the rectangle she formed with her digits, Pandæmonium eagerly described what she wanted the girl to do.

"Won't you please show me a wonderful movie about friendship?"

Akari couldn't respond.

She had said it before. She had thought it, too. Menou was more important to her than the rest of the world, and she didn't care if she had to destroy the world if it meant saving Menou's life, she thought.

And yet.

Akari wrapped her arms around herself. She couldn't stop her body from trembling.

A third of the population of the world? It was beyond imagining.

A nation's worth of land? How many more lives would that mean?

Half of a continent? There was no way she could do such a thing.

The huge number of deaths required for her to go back was horrific. Akari couldn't justify destroying that many lives so she could survive. Even if she could convince herself she was willing, she wouldn't be able to reach out and take it.

Akari had never once claimed a life.

She wasn't nearly so unhinged as to be genuinely willing to enact a plan that would destroy the world, much less kill a considerable number of people with her own hands.

Akari Tokitou was a good person.

"...Mm."

Pandæmonium's voice lost its luster.

The enthusiasm was fading fast from her young eyes. It was as if she was watching a movie that seemed exciting and flashy from the trailers but was obviously mediocre within the first ten minutes. She lowered her hands and let her arms dangle.

Her eyes showed her disinterest without needing to put it into words, finding Akari lacking.

The girl with the Pure Concept *Time* wouldn't become a

source of chaos in this world. She was willing to sacrifice herself, but she couldn't bring carnage to the planet. That much was clear now.

Pandæmonium clasped her hands behind her back and turned away, her white dress fluttering.

"Mm, I should've known."

With that, all thoughts of Akari left her mind completely.

She was already thinking about the next movie.

Casting aside a disappointing film, the source of all *Evil* left the train car before anyone could stop her.

Pandæmonium was gone.

The Director, who'd been sitting next to her, never spoke up once to interrupt the sequence of events.

Pandæmonium's lighthearted words had utterly broken Akari Tokitou's heart. The girl's whispered words destroyed Akari's conviction that she would do anything for the sake of friendship.

Casting a pained glance at the girl who had lost all will to fight, the Director addressed the person he was already acquainted with instead.

"Well, that was certainly chilling. She's normally on her best behavior when she's with Miss Manon... Aren't you going after her, Flare? She made some rather remarkable claims."

"What would be the point of chasing something that won't die and is only a tiny portion of the whole? If Manon Libelle was there, I'd be willing to capture her, but it would be pointless to try to apprehend a pinky finger alone."

There was no point in catching this part of Pandæmonium.

That did make sense. She had probably allowed Pandæmonium to stay here so she would crush the hopes of the girl with the Pure Concept of *Time.*

"So what do you want?"

"Ah yes... Hrmm. Well, you see, Flare..."

The Director glanced at the Master's face hesitantly. Frankly, it was disturbing. What was a man over fifty years old hesitating about? He tapped his foot a few times, clacking his heel against the floor, before he gathered his resolve and looked up.

"I wonder if you and I could start over?"

"Die."

"Oooh?!"

Master Flare threw her scripture at him. It boasted more than five hundred pages and was even reinforced with metal, making it a considerably heavy object. Having it tossed at him at such a short distance made the Director sweat.

"What was that for...? I—I could've been seriously hurt!"

"Next time something creepy and misleading comes out of your mouth, I'll knock you out cold... Ah, you can just burn that old thing. It's been around long enough, hasn't it? Go ahead and torch it."

"Ha-ha... No, thank you."

The Director laughed wryly and handed the scripture back.

He was one of the very few people who knew what scriptures really were.

"I suppose it was a little late for that proposal... Say, Flare. I met your successor."

"Oh yeah?"

"And then there's this girl... Akari Tokitou, was it? The

relationship between this lost lamb of *Time* and your apprentice, Flarette... It's quite similar to you and that friend of yours,
long ago."

"You're imagining things."

Flare and the Director had known each other long enough
that they discussed things with ease, sparing no moment before
replying.

"Say, Flare. How many people do you suppose are aware
of the truth of this world? How many have become twisted
because they learned that truth? The function of the scriptures given to priestesses, the real identity of the Lord, the
history of the Elders... Many people have upon learning these
things."

Earnestness shone in the Director's tone. However, Master
Flare's expression didn't change as she listened.

"Experion, the strongest knight, stopped thinking and
yielded to the Elders. The monster Genom Cthulha holed up
in the eastern Wild Frontier to become an ally of the Mechanical Society, of all things. The great holy woman Ms. Orwell lost
sight of the proper path and gave in to the taboo. I was taken
with the delusion of a great rebellion against the world. And
then...there is you, Master Flare." The Director paused to take a
breath, then posed his question. "How have you been altered?"

"Not at all?"

The answer was immediate.

"I don't remember changing in the least. I have been an Executioner since long ago, and I still am."

"Precisely. You are the one person who chose never to shift.
You decided that was the only way to atone to her, didn't you?"

"Bah-ha-ha!" Master Flare guffawed. She threw her head

back, opened her mouth wide, and burst out with derisive laughter. It was the same mocking sound she reserved for worthless taboos and people who didn't interest her.

"Forget it, Director. If that's all you wanted to talk about, you should've just stayed in your cell. In the end, you can't change a single damn thing. That's all there is to it."

"...I see."

The Director grasped the brim of his bowler hat and pulled it back on, covering his eyes.

He knew better than anyone that he was dwelling on old regrets. Even so, he doggedly persisted, asking another question.

"Could you not at least call me by my name?"

"I think not. I won't waste my breath on the name of some stupid animal."

"I see... But you're not going to kill me, hmm?"

"Lucky you." Master Flare didn't so much as bother drawing her Executioner's blade. "The *Lord* has already forgiven your sin. Isn't that right...*Elder* Director?"

"...Yes, I suppose so."

There was a hint of sadness in the Director's voice as he acknowledged Flare's words.

The speech he'd thrown at Menou in their alleyway encounter was coming back to bite him.

Because of what he knew, he could no longer act. He understood enough to comprehend that he couldn't do anything about it. And what made it even worse was that he still didn't wish he had never learned these things.

The Director stood up.

He'd come to check in on an old acquaintance, wanting to

know what she was like now that she had taken an apprentice. That was his only business here. It was little more than a minor detour; he hadn't been conceited enough to think he might be able to change her.

If there was anyone who could have done as much for Flare, it would have been that one person, twenty years ago, for only a brief time.

The young woman who had the Pure Concept of *Light*.

"What comes next, hmm...?"

The Director left the train car and slowly walked across the platform.

He couldn't do anything anymore. The moment he gained the right to change the world, which he thought was all he wanted, it all seemed unbearably pointless.

So when the girl called Manon appeared before him, he'd followed her. Instead of acting on his own, he thought he could at least assist her without letting his desires mix in, or at least that was how he excused his conduct to himself.

Master Flare would not change. As an Executioner, she was already complete.

"But you know, Flare..."

The Director stopped abruptly.

A lone girl was running through the station—a priestess with her light-chestnut hair tied in a black scarf ribbon.

Their eyes met.

She knew who he was. But evidently, she was short on time, because she didn't stop to make a scene and just kept dashing farther into the station.

As he watched her run determinedly out of sight, his eyes narrowed.

"I don't think the same can be said of your apprentice just yet."

The Director's quiet words were full of hope for the "next" who had finally arrived.

Menou spotted the Director in the station, but she had no time for him. Ignoring his presence, she continued searching for Akari. As she looked around the station, she spotted something clearly out of place: a special Faust convoy train.

It was such an unexpected and ostentatious sight that Menou was almost more impressed than surprised. After all, this was a highly exclusive train with the right to override any schedule. They were only dispatched for exceptional occasions, like when the archbishop was traveling.

How did she manage to get ahold of it? Menou could think of a few methods herself, so she supposed it made sense that her Master would be able to pull it off so easily.

There was no doubt that Akari was inside that train.

Menou had no trouble boarding.

This particular train required very few people to operate. In fact, there was no one else aboard except in the engine room. It truly had been put into motion solely to take Akari to the holy land. There weren't even any guards, enabling Menou to infiltrate it without a hitch.

As she made small talk with the priestesses operating the engine, Menou searched for the optimal path. She had slipped in using Guiding Camouflage to disguise herself. Menou was a member of the Faust, and apparently, Master hadn't given the priestesses any specific information on her. They showed no distrust toward Menou.

Once she was inside, there was no point hiding any longer. Menou openly walked to the next train car and opened the door.

"What's up, Menou?"

Master Flare wasn't surprised to see Menou burst into the room without permission. She didn't seem hostile at all, never mind murderous. She offered Menou a wave without rising from her seat.

"It's been a while. Did you need something?"

"I'm here…" Menou smiled thinly and pointed at Akari, who was sitting across from the Master. "…to pick up that idiot."

"Is that right?"

Master nodded coolly. If anything, it was Akari who looked flustered.

"Well, too bad. You'll have to hand over the Akari Tokitou assignment."

"May I ask why you would take my mission from me?"

"What's it matter to you?"

"I've been her companion all this time, and I intend to see my plan through to the end."

"Her *companion*, eh…?"

Master Flare trailed off meaningfully, but Menou didn't falter, her gaze unwavering.

"The reason for the takeover is simple," Flare continued. "Akari Tokitou has fooled you."

Akari had memories of all the previous time lines she'd regressed. Flare explained that this meant the Otherworlder had been deceiving Menou and influencing her actions.

"We can't leave this in the hands of someone so easily deceived. Even Momo's unsanctioned actions were better. At least she deduced Akari Tokitou's true intentions."

It was a perfect excuse. Sensing that she wouldn't be able to object on reasonable grounds, Menou changed tactics.

"If that's the case, could you let me ride with you by any chance? I was thinking of taking a rest in the holy land once the Akari Tokitou mission is finished."

"Since when are you enough of a big shot for that?" Master Flare responded flatly. "This locomotive's only supposed to be used by people who rival the archbishop in status. I can't let the likes of you on board."

Then why was a Master like Flare allowed to use the train? The woman seemed content not to address that contradiction.

"If you're going to the holy land, you can walk."

She obviously wasn't going to make this easy. Menou sighed; she should've expected as much.

"One more thing, Menou. I'm planning to give you a new job anyway."

"A new job?"

"There's a city nearby that took catastrophic damage from an Original Sin taboo. Pandæmonium and Manon Libelle laid waste to the place on a whim. Go help them rebuild. No hidden agendas, just pure, charitable work helping people." Master crossed her legs and smirked. "You like that kinda thing, right?"

Charitable work.

It was an appropriate role for any other clergy member and far removed from that of an Executioner.

It was strange timing to be given a job like that, but Menou only nodded expressionlessly.

"Very well."

"Good. You do that."

"But...could I talk to this girl one last time? I have all kinds of complaints built up, and I'd love to give her a piece of my mind."

"Do what you want."

The Master gave permission. What's more, she even stood up from her seat.

Menou's eyes widened. Master Flare wasn't going to keep watch on them?

"Master?"

"I have no interest in hearing some insipid discussion."

With that, Master Flare left the two of them in the train car.

Just like that, they were alone.

Menou sat down next to Akari, who watched her with her head still hanging low.

Master Flare had appeared, and Menou came to chase Akari down. That only poured salt on the wound in Akari's spirit.

"Menou…" After sitting in silence for so long, she finally spoke up. "Just leave me alone."

"What are you whining about? You're the one who ran off on your own."

"I don't know. I don't know, so just leave me here."

"Momo told me all about it. So you had your memories, hmm?"

Akari felt something in her chest ache. Whether she was aware of that or not, Menou crossed her legs as she continued.

"You really pulled one over on me. You must've felt like quite the mastermind manipulating me like that, didn't you? Although, I suppose I'm the bigger fool for not figuring it out."

She knew. Menou had found out everything Akari was trying to hide.

But it wasn't too late, not yet.

Akari clenched her fists, which had been resting on her knees.

Whatever the reason, Master Flare wasn't trying to kill Menou this time. To be precise, she had come to collect Akari before Menou could fully betray the Faust.

Akari didn't know the Master's real motives. But as long as she didn't try to save Akari now, Menou still had a chance to survive. Akari made her voice sharper than necessary, trying to act cruelly toward the other girl.

"All the more reason to leave me, then. I finally have the chance to save you…!" Akari could feel her emotions spilling out of her now. "Honestly, it's taken long enough. I repeated everything over and over. And now I've finally done it. So just go away already! How can I solve anything if I depend on you?! It won't fix a single thing!"

"So you decided to hide this from me because asking me for help wouldn't solve anything? That's awfully self-centered."

"I know it is!" Akari's face was bright red as she went on earnestly. "It can't all work out fine in the end, okay? Your Master just told me so. There's a way to go back to Japan and preserve memories, but it'd be better if there wasn't. I know now that it's better this way…!"

She tried to put on a strong front to drive Menou away. "So you don't have to bother with me anymore, Menou. You're always trying to save other people, save *me*…and then you die. Do you think I'm grateful for that…? Don't be ridiculous. No one would want a friend to perish for their sake! I *really* don't want you to disappear, Menou!"

Akari didn't know if it was right or wrong. She just kept

blurting out how she really felt. "It's not *my* fault I repeated things so many times. It's because you're always trying to sacrifice yourself, Menou! Just leave me alone! You're the last person who should be calling me self-centeeEEEEK?!"

Her nearly incoherent rant was interrupted with a shriek.

Menou had grabbed her cheek and gave it a firm tug.

"Listen, Akari. Let me ask you something. Why did these previous instances of me, or whatever, save your life? Has it ever occurred to you that you're just getting a big head by assuming it was for your sake?"

"I-it wasn't?"

"It wasn't."

Menou leaned in closer.

"It's because you tried to protect *me*."

Akari and Momo both had the wrong idea.

After hearing Akari's tale, Momo had reached the same conclusion: Menou betrayed the Faust because of her friendship with Akari. It was always a possibility that Menou would let her emotions cloud her judgment.

Except that wasn't true, because Menou didn't value herself enough to act based on her feelings.

"Look, Akari, I'm a villain."

Menou was ever aware of the countless awful deeds she'd committed. The bloodstained footsteps she'd left in her wake.

That was all the more reason.

"Listen, Akari. I can't have anyone trying to sacrifice themselves for me. Do you know why I became an Executioner? I don't think you do." Menou thought of the time in her childhood when she chose this path. "I did it to save everyone else."

Menou was a wicked person. Throughout her life, she'd killed many people. She'd chosen that way of life.

There was no point in anyone trying to protect someone as villainous as her. She couldn't stand the thought of another risking their life for hers, worthless as it was.

"I refuse to let anyone die to save a monster like me."

Even if that meant she had to die.

That was the only motive that had driven Menou to death so many times before.

Menou released Akari's stretchy cheek, which snapped back into place. Akari rubbed the stinging spot automatically.

"Menou…"

"Yes?"

"You're…actually pretty weird, aren't you?"

"Be quiet."

"Ouch!"

Menou calmly flicked Akari on the forehead.

Then she smiled as Akari clutched her head in pain.

"That's fine by me."

Menou stood up. Sensing that they were about to part ways, Akari stood up, too, and Menou produced something from her pocket that Akari had forgotten.

A headband, decorated with a white flower.

Menou placed the gift she'd been pressed into buying for Akari on the girl's head and lightly brushed her hair into place.

"I'll need some time to prepare to come after you, so it'll take a little while…but be a good girl and wait for me this time, understood?"

If Akari shook her head, would Menou give up?

©nilitsu

She thought there might be a sliver of hope, but as soon as she met Menou's eyes, she knew it was impossible.

"...Okay."

Akari nodded meekly and touched a hand to her headband. Menou was looking right at her—and her alone.

There was no refusing when Menou had that glint in her eyes. Akari had to concede that there was no winning against the other girl.

"I'll be waiting for you, Menou."

The pair exchanged a promise that would lead them into the future while alone on the train.

There was just one thing Menou didn't tell Akari.

The reason she betrayed the Faust in previous time lines and shook off any guilt about it. Perhaps her inability to accept another's aid for a villain like her was part of it, but it wasn't the only reason.

It was because she knew the punishment for that crime perfectly well.

"What, you're alone?" Master Flare remarked when Menou disembarked from the car.

"Yes, of course. I didn't bring Momo with me."

The Master smirked without a word. Obviously, that wasn't what she meant.

It didn't look like Master Flare was going to kill Menou now. After all, she wasn't a traitor yet. Flare wouldn't execute anyone without concrete proof that they had committed a taboo worthy of execution. And Menou genuinely wasn't planning on stealing Akari back here. She wasn't foolhardy enough to try to do something like that right under her Master's nose without any preparation.

Flare was an Executioner to her core.

And to Menou, that was a relief.

If Menou turned traitor, or made a mistake, or stooped to the taboo... The moment she stepped off her path as an Executioner, she knew there was someone who would bring her the proper punishment.

No matter how much she prepared, how hard she resisted, she could never win. No matter how far she fled, she could never escape. An unbelievable, unshakable force in the shape of a person would always find her.

Menou could genuinely believe that a power akin to divine punishment would penalize her accordingly if she did something wrong.

It was a great comfort to know her crimes would be punished appropriately.

"Well, if you'll excuse me."

As Menou tried to play dumb to the very end, Master Flare stopped her with a relaxed smile.

"Really, you should've just taken her and run away now. You're far too cautious. I suppose you see me as a monster like Pandæmonium or something."

"No, of course not."

Her denial wasn't a lie. She didn't think Master Flare was on par with Pandæmonium.

In Menou's mind, the name Flare ranked far higher.

Whatever meaning the Master took from Menou's response, she opened her mouth wide and laughed.

"You know, Menou. I'm not immortal, nor am I invincible. There are only two conjuring crests in this dagger. All I have besides that is a scripture. The only special skill I have to speak of is Guiding Camouflage, but it seems you've been catching up to me in that department, too."

Menou was very familiar with the conjurings Master had on hand.

Everything she was had been drilled into Menou's mind. In terms of battle strategies, there was almost nothing that her pupil Menou didn't already know about.

"As for Guiding Force, I have less than even Momo, never mind an Otherworlder. In that respect, I'm not much different from you. It's been a while since I retired, so my body's gone softer, too. My stamina can't compare with a youngster like you. Getting old is the worst, you know."

In a sense, this was probably true. There really was very little difference between their levels of capability.

"I'm not strong in the least."

Why was it, then, that the more she spoke frankly about her own weakness, the mightier she seemed?

"And you, on the other hand? From the sound of things, you've taken on some pretty big fish in the past few months. Orwell, who was one of the best conjurers of the Faust and earned the seat of archbishop. The pinky finger of Pandæmonium, one of the Four Major Human Errors. The Primary Color conjured soldier that the Mechanical Society created. That's a damned impressive lineup. Even in my heyday, I hardly ever fought such strong enemies head-on. No doubt I'm far weaker than any of them."

She was listing Menou's accomplishments since she met Akari. They had certainly all been dramatic upsets. Few people could have faced such adversaries alone and lived to tell the tale.

"Now that you've grown so much, I'm sure I couldn't beat you in a fight."

Her teacher was speaking the truth.

She was weaker than the taboos Menou had fought thus far. In terms of pure power, she might've been the lowest ranked opponent Menou had faced recently. There was a decent chance of beating her.

At the same time, that didn't mean much in Menou's opinion. The unpleasant feeling in her chest showed on her face in the form of a grim smile.

"However...," Menou began. "I'm sure you could have killed them all, Master."

Menou had failed to slay them. Pandæmonium was still alive. Menou had thought Manon and Sahara dead, too, yet they both escaped death after committing taboos. What's more, Menou hadn't defeated Archbishop Orwell on her own, either.

Master Flare said nothing. Her disinterested-looking eyes, if nothing else, were the same as they had always been.

As far as Menou was concerned, Master Flare was the most formidable opponent in the world.

"Master."

"What?"

"Right now, I think I'm trying to take the wrong path in life."

"I see."

"I said that I wanted to be like you, and now I'm attempting to do so."

The hometown where Menou began and the journey she'd traveled alongside the priestess with the dark-red hair had somehow become distant memories. At first, she'd constantly been comparing her present to the past, but now she hardly thought back on it.

Menou's time with her Master was her core.

However, what surfaced most vividly in her heart now was her haphazard adventure with Akari, retracing the steps of that first journey.

"I know I can still make the right choice, for now. But even so…" Menou knew she had a choice, and so she stared intently at her red-haired teacher. "I'm going to become that pure, noble, strong, and villainous priestess."

At that, Master Flare threw back her head and laughed.

"You really are a fool."

"Well…yes." Menou's grin turned wry. "I'm perfectly aware of that myself."

There was no refuting that.

Master Flare turned her back on Menou and entered the car. Before long, the train began to move. The Guiding engine started up, producing sparkling Guiding Light. As Menou followed the Guiding Light trailing behind the last train with her eyes as it receded into the distance, she found herself gazing up at the sky.

It was bisected into two colors: crimson and indigo. These opposite hues clashed intensely overhead. Slowly, the red gave way to the dark blue, and finally, the stars began to shine, breathtakingly beautiful.

Akari and Master Flare's train was long out of sight.

MATO SATO

While Menou gazed at the tracks leading forward and the dazzling sky above, Menou thought about the endless road ahead and whispered, "I really…don't want to die."

She squinted as she peered into the distance, searching for her way of life.

The train stopped at a platform covered in white.

Pilgrims from all over the world visited this place, and members of the Faust were required to make the trip at least once in their lives. This was the holy land.

The lone station in that city was off-limits to ordinary citizens. It was rarely used at all, since there was no regular schedule.

A priestess with dark-red hair disembarked from the locomotive.

Someone came to welcome her back to the holy land, from which she'd been absent for about a month.

"...So you're finally here."

A tall, spindly old woman glared at the Master; her voice had a vigor that defied her age. Her elegant yet pure robes indicated she was in the position of archbishop.

Archbishop Elcami was one of the most famous names in the world. However, while most people knew she was the archbishop who safeguarded the holy land, few were aware that she was also an Elder.

Now she held her scripture in arms that had grown skinny with age, glowering at the Master with her commanding eyes.

"I assume you have an excuse for persistently avoiding any form of contact, Master Flare."

"Sorry about that, Magician. But you already know, right?"

Flare looked irritable as ever, even though she was dealing with someone who could very well be described as one of the most powerful people in the world. She waved her scripture in the air impatiently.

"This scripture is broken."

Elcami, also called the Magician, furrowed her brow at the apparent excuse.

She swallowed the automatic urge to bellow in response and took a deep breath, responding in a low groan instead.

"...Fine, whatever. Well? Were you able to capture *Time*?"

"Yeah, it's in the train. I'm sure it'll come out soon enough. You can take it away then."

"What of Manon Libelle and Pandæmonium? You encountered them as well, did you not?"

"What about them? They got away. I don't know what they're up to. Doing whatever they please, I'm sure."

"You incompetent louse! You couldn't even finish off one little girl?!"

The aged woman really did shout with a remarkably thunderous voice for her age, but the Master only shrugged.

She didn't look sorry in the least. Elcami clicked her tongue in frustration.

"Don't get ahead of yourself just because of who dwells in your scripture."

"Like I care. It's nothing but a pain as far as I'm concerned."

"How dare you…!"

Her eyes raged as if she were about to breathe fire. Still looking unrepentant, the Master looked away.

"See, there you go. That's Akari Tokitou."

The black-haired girl who emerged from the car glared silently at the two before her.

Her eyes looked defiant. After Pandæmonium had crushed her spirit, she'd seemed listless for a while, but something had swiftly revived her. Akari's attitude was so rebellious that it was surprising she hadn't tried to escape on the way here.

"All we have to do is use the Sword of Salt on her, and it'll all be over. Is the teleport gate ready to go there?"

"…It'll take a week to prepare. Remain on standby until then."

"That's a long time. You couldn't set it up in advance?"

"We only have so many personnel who can operate the gate. Not to mention, few people are allowed to know about this plan. Add *your* unpredictable actions into the mix, and how could I possibly calculate it beforehand?!"

"I see. Sounds rough."

As Elcami raged at her, Flare stared back coolly, as if to keep raising the Elder's blood pressure until she died.

Archbishop Elcami, the protector of the holy land, was also known as Elder Magician.

Although her title sounded like something out of a fairy tale, her personality was much more pragmatic. She was so underhanded and narrow-minded that it was a wonder she'd risen to the rank of archbishop.

Or perhaps, ironically enough, it was her awareness of her own failings that prevented her from straying down the same path as Orwell.

"A week, huh…?"

The Master repeated the length of time aloud as she watched Elcami walk away with Akari in tow.

This version of Menou had the same look in her eyes as a Menou from another time.

"A new conjuring…? You had me bring Akari all the way here… for something like that…?"

"That's right."

"…I see."

Master Flare's exchange with the very first Menou surfaced in her mind. When her apprentice brought Akari to the holy land and discovered how the Pure Concept of *Time* was to be used there, she turned traitorous.

So there was little doubt that she would come this time.

"All right, Menou."

The red-haired woman's mouth twisted sardonically.

They had done this over and over by now. The reset point was always Menou's death. They'd allowed this to keep happening so that the Pure Concept of *Time* would keep forfeiting memories, which would eventually allow them to harvest the concept and make it a new conjuring.

They were already plenty far enough along. One last push, and Akari Tokitou would turn into a Human Error.

"There won't be a next time."

Master Flare knew that this round of killing her apprentice would be the last.

Menou was busily preparing to depart.

She returned to the hotel, told Ashuna they would be going their separate ways, and moved to the inn where Momo was staying. There, as she repacked her belongings, Momo called to her in a quavering voice.

"Um, darling…"

"Yes?"

"You *are* going to the city Master assigned you to, aren't you?"

"What? No." Menou's response was immediate. "I'm going to the holy land. There are plenty of other people who can help rebuild that town."

"B-but…you're just going back for a rest, then, right?"

"Of course not… You can stay behind, you know."

"…No, I'll come with yooou."

"Oh? Don't tell me you feel sorry for Akari now?"

"That would never happen. I want to come for *your* sake, darling."

Menou was only teasing, but Momo responded with a poutier look than necessary. Realizing based on her deep knowledge of Momo's personality that she might've actually hit the nail on the head, Menou was surprised and a little touched.

"Say, Momo."

"What is it, darling?"

"How do you think conjurings are created?"

"Er…"

Momo looked taken aback by the unexpected change in topic.

It was the same question Akari had asked her not long before. Momo frowned as she responded.

"Well… I'm not sure."

"I see."

Menou was starting to figure it out.

After speaking with Manon, seeing how Sahara transformed from the influence of the Mechanical Society, and most
of all her conversation with Master Flare and the truth that
Akari revealed, she was all but certain.

"I think conjurings must come about in some truly awful
way."

"Oh...really?"

"Yes. I'm quite sure of it."

Ever since Momo told her that Akari had used *Regression* on
the world countless times while retaining her memories, Menou
had been thinking about something.

Master Flare would never fail repeatedly at assassinat-
ing a single Pure Concept holder. Even if Akari was immortal
and wielded a conjuring that turned back time, Master would
undoubtedly find a way to get around that and execute her.

That meant that Master was allowing Akari to turn back
time repeatedly with some specific goal in mind. There had to
be a reason she permitted it.

What exactly led to the birth of a new conjuring?

Guiding Force was a power that existed in every living thing.

Did humanity acquire conjurings by experimenting with
the use of that power?

If the order of events was to be believed, that was likely not
the answer.

All that the residents of this world had mastered on their
own was Guiding Enhancement. The concept of "conjurings"
probably didn't exist at first.

"The source of conjurings is the Pure Concepts that Otherworlders have."

Pure Concepts.

Original Sin Concepts, the Concept of Primary Colors, crest conjurings, and scripture conjurings… All of them were brought about by the Otherworlders who came to this world.

Menou didn't know how or why they started being summoned to this planet in the first place.

Yet ever since Otherworlders had started to arrive, concepts attached to their souls by way of Guiding Force and were established as Pure Concepts in the form of conjurings that the Otherworlders could subconsciously use.

The concepts embedded in their souls were torn away when they lost control and became Human Errors. As soon as this happened, the concept contained within a single human became omnipresent in the world as a conjuring phenomenon.

That was why the Master had let Momo do as she pleased. Momo's efforts to make Akari keep using her Pure Concept worked perfectly for her.

Master Flare's goal was for Akari to turn into a Human Error.

She wanted the Pure Concept of *Time* to become accessible to the world through time conjurings.

According to Momo, when Menou first reached the land of salt, she'd tried to save Akari and died to her Master.

But that couldn't be right.

She must have tried to kill Akari instead.

If Akari was going to turn into a Human Error, it would be better for her to perish. Such was the duty of Executioners. Menou's personal feelings and her path in life had coincided enough that she tried to go against her Master's will.

She set foot in that land of salt, believing it would be better if she outwitted her Master and killed Akari with her own hands.

Menou acted out of anger over Akari's attempts to protect her from the second time on. However, that first time, Menou tried to end Akari while she was still Akari—and was executed by her Master for it.

"This world really is hopeless, isn't it?"

Menou produced glowing Guiding Light. She used Guiding Camouflage to manipulate it and form a projected map of the continent.

The light of Guiding Force...

This luminous phenomenon was called Guiding Light because it glowed in the darkness.

Menou understood the term's etymology, but she suggested an alternate interpretation of her own.

"This power surely exists to guide Otherworlders...the lost ones."

Menou hadn't given up when she'd watched that train haul Akari away.

She was only just getting started.

All Menou could do for anyone, no matter how hard she tried—getting covered in mud, bathing in blood, using every means available, and with the worst of intent—was to kill them.

Still, she would cut open the path to a new way of life for them.

"Let's go, Momo."

"Yes, darling."

The Executioner began down the road she hoped would lead to a better existence.

©nilitsu

AFTERWORD

As usual, I owe this volume's existence to the great effort of the illustrator, nilitsu, and the editor, Null, as well as everyone else who supported the book's creation. I'm in a veritable storm of gratitude.

For some reason, the epilogue ends on an "Our fight has only just begun!" kind of note, but please don't worry. The story will continue in Volume 5.

Now, as far as current topics go, I'm sure everyone has been affected by the coronavirus. I hope all of you readers have been getting by all right. As an author who used to name my video game characters Corona in the past, it's certainly a strange feeling to see this name going around. But being a natural-born shut-in otaku who always stays indoors, I thought quarantine would be a piece of cake for me.

...It's much harder than I expected.

*   *   *

Having to refrain from most kinds of recreation can be pretty difficult. As of this writing, the pandemic shows no signs of letting up anytime soon, so please take good care of yourselves so you don't build up too much stress.

But since we all have to stay indoors right now anyway, I do have one piece of news that might brighten your day. It's a manga adaptation!

A manga version of *The Executioner and Her Way of Life* by Ryo Mitsuya is launching in *Young Gangan* magazine! It'll kick off the magazine with full-color pages two issues in a row. Sometimes magnificent and sometimes comical, the manga versions of Menou, Akari, Momo, and everyone else are beautifully rendered in every panel. Please be sure to follow the serialization closely!

Having illustrations for a novel I wrote is already the most incredible joy imaginable, and it makes my heart dance every single time.

This is the first time one of my works is getting a manga adaptation, and it's so exciting that I feel like I get to be a fan myself.

I hope we can meet again in Volume 5 of the novels, too.

Until next time!